Sharing the

Sheets

Sharing the Sheets

Natalie Weber

www.urbanbooks.net

Urban Books, LLC
300 Farmingdale Road, NY-Route 109
Farmingdale, NY 11735

ISBN 13: 978-1-62286-538-3
ISBN 10: 1-62286-538-3

First Mass Market Printing October 2017
First Trade Paperback Printing April 2015
Printed in the United States of America

10 9 8 7 6 5 4 3 2 1

Distributed by Kensington Publishing Corp.
Submit orders to:
Customer Service
400 Hahn Road
Westminster, MD 21157-4627
Phone: 1-800-733-3000
Fax: 1-800-659-2436

Sharing the Sheets

Natalie Weber

Acknowledgments

First and foremost I thank God. If it wasn't for Him I would not have the strength to carry on.

Thank you to all my fans, because if there was no love and support, I would be long gone from this game.

I would like to give a special shout to, Carl Weber. You're not just my boss in real life, but my family. Love you like cooked food!

Thanks to my editors, Diane and Clarissa. We got through it once again.

Thanks to the Urban Books team, you guys make it happen.

Lastly, thanks to my boys for understanding the space and time I needed to get this done. I love you unconditionally.

1

Regina

"Come on, we got like two hours. I don't want to waste any time. I need you inside me." I grabbed at his belt to unbuckle it because he was moving too slow for me.

He swatted at my hands.

I sighed. "What is your fucking problem?" My pussy was wet. My nipples were hard as hell. *I was butt-ass naked when I let you in, did you not think I was ready to fuck? That's what I get for thinking there would be no attachments.*

"Damn. I just thought—"

"You thought what?" I asked with a full attitude.

"I thought . . . You know what, forget it. Come on. Where you want it at?"

I flashed him a big-ass smile and his little delay was quickly forgotten. I didn't hesitate to drop to my knees while he unbuckled his belt. In one movement he dropped his pants and boxers exposing his strong ten inches to my face. His smell was fresh and he was neatly trimmed. I licked my lips and took all of him into my wet, warm mouth. His moans soon filled the room. It turned me on even more to hear him groan from my pleasure. I sucked him harder and stronger and just when his moans became louder I stopped. Quickly I got on all fours. "Fuck me," I demanded.

"Oh, you want it like that?"

"What you waiting on? You already got the invite." I was fired up and ready to get my back blown out.

He rammed himself into me to shut me up. I thought I was going to cum after one stroke from him. I clenched my pussy tight every time he entered.

"Ahhh, fuck, you feel so good," he shouted as he tugged on my ponytail.

"Yes, fuck this pussy. Pull it, wrap it tight. Fuck me like a whore," I said wanting him to just go buck wild on me; I wanted it rough and crazy, like the kind of sex where you are even surprised at yourself because you were so excited.

He gave it to me good. He slammed, slapped, and tossed my ass around like a rag doll. Just how I wanted it. Soon we were in my bedroom.

He threw my ass on the bed and that's when I heard a car pull into the driveway. He didn't hear it.

"Stop." He wasn't complying so I pushed him off of me and jumped off the bed. I listened intently.

"Why you stopping me? I thought you—"

"Get under the bed. My husband is home." I grabbed all of his shit and tossed it under the bed and ran out the bedroom. *If his ass ain't get under that bed, both our asses are screwed.* At the time I had no idea how or what was going to happen when I entered the small hallway. I didn't have time to jump into the shower or anything. *Oh well, fuck it. I just won't let him eat me out.*

It was routine for him to go straight to the fridge after walking in. I tiptoed toward the foyer to glance in the mirror to fix my hair because I knew it was a wreck. Then I posted myself leaning against the living room wall facing the kitchen. At first he didn't realize I was there. I watched him close the fridge door and turn around. His eyes finally met my naked body.

"Hi, honey, how was your day?"

He smiled. "It's about to be a whole lot better." He pulled me toward him and gently kissed my neck.

"Ahh, baby, this such a nice surprise." He palmed my ass with his right hand and gently played with my nipple with his left. "Come on, let's go to the bedroom. I got something for you." He started to remove his clothes and dropped them to the floor.

My heart started to beat a little faster. I wasn't about to act nervous and give myself away. I had it good and I wasn't going to fuck it up over some side dick. "Give it to me now, baby. No need for the bed." I tried to lure him away from the thought of needing a bed.

"No, baby, I want to make love to my wife." He picked me up into his arms and carried me into the bedroom.

I was so fucking scared when he laid me on the bed, I could barely breathe correctly.

"Baby, you okay?" my husband asked noticing my sudden hesitation to take in air.

"I'm fine, sweetie. Show me what you got for me." I pulled him closer to me and kissed him passionately. *Fuck it. Tony just gonna have to hear it, moans and all.* "Stick it in me, baby." I pulled on both my nipples and opened my legs wide.

His little thumbsy stood at great attention ready to be swallowed by my gushing river. He was no bigger than six inches, but he sure could eat some pussy and his pockets was never-ending which made up for anything he was lacking.

"Ooh wee, look at my sugar. It's so wet. Was you starting without me?" His fingers passed over my wet opening. "Let me taste some of my honey." He scooted down between my legs like a happy little nerd seeing pussy for the first time.

"No, no, no, I want you now. Put it in me. I need it." I rolled over and cocked my ass in the air. Once I felt his hips against my ass I put on the show, bucking my ass, screaming all types of dirty, nasty shit to get his ass off. It only took a few minutes of embarrassing phrases that Tony would definitely throw back in my face at a later date. I didn't care. This just had to be over with in a hurry.

"Turn over. Pull your legs back."

I flipped onto my back and pulled my ankles to the back of my ears. He slipped himself into one of my holes. At that point I really didn't give a shit which hole he stuck it into just as long as his thumbsy ass got off and I could get Tony's ass out of my house.

With a few more thrusts it was over. Immediately I wiggled from under him thinking of Tony down below. "Don't tell me that's all you have. Let's go take a shower. I want you to control those new power streams we just got installed." I winked and hopped off the bed. I bent over and shook my butt so he didn't have a reason to pass up the offer. I closed my eyes and slowly headed to the bathroom. I started to count silently, *one, two, thr* . . . Then there it was: the sound of him easing off the bed. *Thank goodness.*

"I'm right behind that fat ass." He ran up behind me and smacked my ass hard.

All I was thinking about was getting his ass in there. I was definitely going to keep his ass in there for a while. *Shit, that stupid motherfucker, Tony, probably won't get the hint!* I hurried into the bathroom, heading straight to the shower. I opened the glass door and Mark was right behind me.

"Ooh, baby, do you want your little friend to play?" I'd been neglecting his needs so I knew this would get me back in the room for a quick second.

"Yeah, let me go—"

I latched on to his biceps. "No, baby, let me go get it. Besides I want to make an entrance. Just tap on those buttons and get it steamy in here. Get ready for me, big boy." I let his arm go and exited the shower. "I'll be right back. Don't you follow me, you'll ruin the surprise."

"Hurry your ass up then," he said with a chuckle.

I rushed out the bathroom door and closed it quickly behind me. I didn't see Tony. I panicked; I dove to the floor, raised the bed curtain, and looked under the bed. I whispered, "Tony. Tony."

Suddenly a wet touch hit my ass crack. I jumped and knocked my head against the bottom of the king-sized bed. "Fuck!" When I turned around Tony was standing over me stroking his manhood and licking his lips. Oh, damn, there was only one answer for that pose. It was pure lust and symptoms of a whore-like mental disorder that filled my body. I jumped up and ran to the bathroom door. I held on to the doorknob and bent over. As I looked back at him I whispered, "Just a few strokes then get your clothes out the hallway closet and get the fuck out."

For the next three minutes he pushed into my flesh like a bucking bull. *Damn, that shit feels so fucking good.* "Tony, enough." I stood up still holding on to the doorknob and turned around with Tony still wanting more. "Move your ass. My husband has two guns in this bed-room alone. I don't think you want to die with the label 'rapist' on your headstone. Trust me he would." With those words his movement became urgent. I didn't even get a good-bye kiss. I laughed to myself.

Now back to the matter at hand. Feeling more comfortable that Tony was gone I walked over to my armoire and opened it. I pulled out my eight-inch strap-on and got it on. I took a tube of KY jelly out and squirted some onto the head of my new dick. *Yes, baby, here I come. This should earn me a few days of alone time.* The thought of the reward after fucking him in the ass was enough for me to get off. Without any hesitation I headed into back into the bathroom to do my husband right.

2

Mark

The bathroom was nice and steamy just like Regina loved it. With all these new jet streams in the shower it proved to be the right call to renovate the condo. Damn, she was taking long. I didn't know how much longer I could keep that woody.

Just when my little man was about to go limp, the bathroom door opened. I tugged on my dick to keep me hard. I needed someone else to be in control for the moment. I wasn't gay and only allowed Regina to fuck me in my ass and get me out of my structured, planned life. It was only this past year that our sex life became over the top when it happened.

"You ready, daddy?" The shower door opened. She stood there all strapped up and ready to dedicate.

Daddy? Since when has she ever used that ghetto-ass terminology? "Daddy?" I gave her an odd look.

"Yes. Aren't you the one who provides for me, gives me everything I need?" She rubbed on her new member.

"Well, please keep it behind closed doors." I didn't like that shit and I wasn't going to mislead her that I favored her endearment.

"Sorry, baby, it won't happen again." She fixed her best puppy-eyed, "lost my best friend," "I'm so sorry" look on but it didn't work.

I grabbed her by the strap-on and unbuckled it. She tried at first to stop me but must've realized I had something to prove to her. As a man I wasn't about to let her fuck me in my ass after calling me daddy. "Get on the bench and open those legs real wide." I held the strap-on in my hands and walked over to the system pad by the glass door. I tapped a button twice and a stream of water shot out the ceiling over the bench. Regina knew exactly what to do; she fixed her goods directly under the shooting water. She opened her legs wide and exposed her clit to the fullest. As soon as the stream hit her moans were heard.

"Yes, baby. Oh shit. Come fuck your pussy, baby."

With those words I did as commanded. I walked back over, took a seat at the end of the bench, and watched her excitement climax. I took a look at my little man standing at attention and the eight-inch cock in my hand; I opted on using the eight inches. Her eyes widened with surprise when I slid it into her gently. I knew my dick wasn't big, but she would never know *I* thought so. There's just some things a man will never admit to anyone; it works out better if you just to play the game.

"Wow, baby, it's so big it hurts . . . but good. Shit that's good."

I knew she wasn't lying. For the past eight years she only had me in her. If it didn't hurt I would have to question her in the worst way. It took a minute to get all eight inches into her, but by her screams of pleasure I knew it wasn't hurting that bad. As she continued to climax from the continuous jet stream of water on her clit and me fucking her hard with the strap-on my smaller head started to throb. I was about to bust. I left the strap-on in her and stood up. I held my manhood and directed straight to her mouth. She took all of me. It was one of the best feelings in the world to me; busting all my juice into her warm, wet mouth made me cum harder. It almost made me cum again instantly.

"Ahhhhh. Damn, baby, that was so good," I said out of breath. She sucked every last drop of my love juice out of me.

"Don't stop please, baby. I want to come again. Mmm . . ." The pulsating, jet-propelled water was still doing its main purpose: giving her the time of her life over and over again. She was now in a sitting position with her back slightly arched. Regina took ahold of the strap-on and did as she pleased with it, moving it in and out of her vigorously as the water came down faster in tempo.

I watched her cum again, then moved over to one of the bigger showerheads and washed off. I took pleasure in pleasing her no matter the cost. After cleaning myself off I exited the shower leaving her to go numb in a world of unstoppable bliss. I dried off and threw my robe on. After stepping into my room, there it was: another fucking bridal magazine on the dresser and on my side.

Ever since we moved back in after the renovation, the in-your-face hints had been on full blast. I don't understand women. When we first met, I told her I didn't believe a document or a big fancy party had to prove I wanted to spend the rest of my life with someone. It was a waste of money if you asked me; inviting tons of people and only 10 percent of them actually reach in their pockets to offer a gift. They do what most guests do at any wedding: eat their bellies full, get wasted and, if you're single, straight to the hotel with someone else who's as drunk and horny as you are.

I'd shared my life with Regina for eight years; didn't she know we're already considered married? She didn't have a need for anything. I treated her like my wife on paper, public, and private: her name was on everything, I referred to her as my wife in any and every form there was, and adored her as my queen beside me. I just didn't understand why after all this time she wanted to actually get married. I shook my head and picked up the magazine, flipped through the pages, and tossed it to her side of the dresser. The way I saw it, if she asked me about it I wouldn't be lying when I said yes.

The echoes from the bathroom told me she was going to be awhile. I took the opportunity to get some work done. I slipped into my flip-flops and headed to the kitchen. Glancing at the digital clock on the microwave, I picked up my cell phone off the counter. 2 Missed Calls flashed across the screen. *Shit, that was the fucking call I was waiting for. Fuck it, it's only nine o'clock out West.* I tapped the screen and put the phone on speaker.

"Hey, Mark, thanks for getting back to me," a deep voice answered.

"So, Steve, do we have a deal at $3.5 million, fully furnished, all cash?" I crossed my fingers like a schoolgirl, but my tone was firm and quick.

"Can we close in ten days?" he asked.

"Congratulations, I will have the contract to you shortly. Next time you're in town we'll get together."

"Definitely, we'll talk soon." Seconds later the phone disconnected.

"Yes!" I shouted and freely spun around resulting in one of Michael Jackson's infamous poses.

"What got you Billie Jean-ing?" I heard a giggle.

"Just closed the deal on that one-bedroom on the Lower East Side." I was happy I kept a laptop in the kitchen. I rarely stepped into my home office now that there's a room for it. I opened the laptop and quickly went to work on the contract.

"I can't believe somebody actually brought that place. That neighborhood sucks."

"Now don't tell me you thought I wouldn't be able to sell it?" I stopped typing and waited for an answer.

"Never, you are the best at what you do. You just listed it about a week ago. I just didn't think you would sell it that fast, that's all." She kissed me on the lips and walked over to the fridge.

"Can you get me a water please?" She placed the bottle next to the laptop. "Thanks. You going to bed or back into the shower?" I smiled naughtily, pulling her close to me.

"I don't know if I can give that addiction up."

Her eyes fluttered just talking about it. I untied her robe and passed my fingers over her clit. She nearly bucked from my arms at the slightest touch.

"Please, baby, no more. I can't . . ."

I picked her up. "I might just have to put a password on that shit so your ass don't get carried away. I don't want to come home one day to find you looking like a prune." I had to laugh while I held her in my arms. I carried her into the bedroom and laid her on the bed.

"Oh shut up. I didn't even know it could do that. I should be mad at you for not showing me that sooner. I'm tired, baby, are you coming to bed soon?"

I kissed her on the forehead and tucked her in. "Yes, I'll be in bed soon. I love you."

"I love you too."

Before I even walked out the room she was snoring. Tomorrow she would unquestionably have some trouble walking. I headed back to the kitchen to finish up the contract. It was a little before one in the morning when I sent the final contract out. I shut off my laptop and cut the lights. I went to bed with a smile on my face.

3

Tony

It had been two days since I saw Regina. I didn't believe she wanted nothing to do with me; she wasn't taking my calls, acknowledging any of my direct messages on FB, or replying to my e-mails. *Did her man find out? We spoke for the past three months close to ten times a day someway somehow. Now she won't even answer me.*

I pulled my dresser drawer out and searched through it until I found it: Regina's red lace thong from our last night together. I held it close to my nose, inhaling her. It still carried her scent, sweet and sexy. She had all I needed and I had to have her. I just didn't want the extra baggage she held on to.

Snapping out my world I stuffed my token of her safely away. I looked to my phone on the bed. I sent another direct message: Now I'm worried. What's going on? I'm on my way.

Hopefully that'd get her attention. I stared at my phone for the next ten minutes. Nothing popped up on the screen. It was one in the morning. *Fuck it, I'm going over there.* As much as I knew that going over there would and could be a huge mistake, I didn't care. I threw on the nearest pair of Nikes, grabbed my car keys, and headed out the door.

I didn't know what it was about Regina, but when I was near her everything in me went numb. The softness of her skin, her lips, her voice; I never felt this way about any woman. Regina had it all: the body—perfect; her mind—limitless; her style—always ahead of the game.

I darted to the car, jumped in, and was so nervous about appearing at her front door at this time, I dropped the keys. I bent my head over the steering wheel and said in a whisper, "What the hell are you doing? She wasn't supposed to get under me like this!"

I picked my head up and reached for my keys on the floor next to the gas pedal. I put the key in the ignition but didn't turn it. Instead I stared through the windshield out at the dim streetlights. It was quiet; hardly anyone was outside. My fingers were still in position to turn the key, but my mind wouldn't allow it.

"She's taken. She isn't yours!" I spoke out loud to nudge myself out the car.

I didn't budge. I covered my eyes with my hands.

Suddenly, my phone buzzed. Meet me @ Hilton off LIE exit 49. Rm 5066. R, rolled across the screen. My eyes opened wider with happiness. I had to look again to make sure I saw correctly. It wasn't her usual number so my contentment abruptly dissipated. *This could be a setup,* crossed my mind. I decided to call the number to make sure it was her.

It rang four times before someone answered: "Why are you calling me? You should be on your way."

A huge grin came across my face. "Baby, my baby, what took you so long to call me? I missed you."

"Tony, we discussed this. It will never be. I love my life; now you can play your part in it or I can get a replacement. Which would you like?"

Her sternness got my dick hard instantly. "Say no more, I'm on my way." I pushed End on the screen, turned the key in the ignition, and put the car in gear. I pushed my foot on the gas and zipped my way to the Long Island Expressway from Midtown Manhattan. My mind was racing. *I thought we had more than just sex. Am I falling in love? Why won't she leave him? He's not her husband, there's no record of a marriage certificate. I know that for a fact. She's not the only one with a high powered friend or two. If she strictly wants sex, then that's exactly what she's going to get—for now. Soon she will be mine. I'll make sure of it.*

Thirty minutes later I was exiting off the highway following the directions from my phone to the Hilton. I drove around the lot looking for Regina's baby blue Bentley. I didn't see it. My paranoia made an appearance again. *This is a fucking setup!* I pulled into a parking space at the back of the hotel. I picked up my phone and exited the navigation on my phone. Searching my call log I called the last number dialed.

"You better be downstairs," Regina answered.

"I am, where's your car?"

"In the shop. Is there a problem?" she questioned.

"Matter of fact, there is." I waited for her response.

Regina's breaths became deeper. "What?"

"I have one question for you: are you setting me up for your man to get at me?"

"You can't be serious. Do you actually think that I—me, someone you fucking on the regular—would do that?" Her tone was no longer sexy.

"Yeah, I do." There was a long pause before she spoke again.

"Listen, Tony, there's no one holding a gun to your head. Do whatever you feel. I'm through."

The phone clicked in my ear. If it was a setup then I was surely dead. *Fuck it. I didn't drive all this way just to turn back.* I knew the room number already so I looked for a back door of the hotel. There was one; I only hoped that I didn't need a key card to enter. *Fuck!* I cursed the key card slot for the door. Suddenly the door opened. *Yes!* I grabbed the handle and held the door.

"Thanks," the man offered.

"No, thank you. Have a good night," I replied and entered the hotel.

I walked straight to the elevator and pushed the call button. I was still kind of nervous, but so far so good. The elevator doors opened and I entered pushing the fifth-floor button. It only took a minute to arrive at the fifth floor. When the doors opened and I cautiously peeked out and quickly reverted my head back. I pushed the fourth floor button instead and exited then. I walked toward the staircase and walked up one flight of stairs. Again, I opened the door and poked my head out. The hallway was empty. I stood there for a minute listening to the dead silence in the air. Slowly I followed the signs to the room number. With a few steps down the long hallway her room was in front of me. Before I knocked, I stepped to the side so she couldn't see me through the peephole.

No answer. I was completely nervous. I slowly moved away from the door. I damn sure didn't want to knock on the door again. I waited for a few seconds then I started to head back to the elevator.

After few steps I heard a door open then her sweet voice filled the air: "Daddy, where you going? I thought you were here to handle your business." She appeared in the hallway butt-ass naked with some spiky, tall heels on.

I almost tripped on my own feet rushing toward her. It took me less than four seconds to have her in my arms. Immediately, I palmed her ass, lifted her off her feet, and pushed my tongue eagerly into her mouth. Her back hit the slightly closed door. I pressed my body against her to push the door open.

Once in the room I gave her a pat on her ass and carried her to the bed. I turned back around to secure the door and hang the Do Not Disturb sign on the outside handle. When I returned to the bed Regina was already started. Her legs were wide open, with her left fingers pulling at her nipple, and with her right hand inserting a dildo fast and steady into her pink deep hole.

"Yes, daddy, please come handle me. I need you in me."

I was undressed in an instant. I was at full attention. Rubbing on my pulsating head, I moved to the edge of the bed closer to the headboard. Her eyes met my ten inches and she devoured it like a pro, moving down slowly allowing her salvia to lubricate her movement.

"Ahh, that feels so good. Yes, call me daddy," I cooed.

She opened her eyes, took me in deeper, and moved the dildo even faster in and out of her flower. I was ready to give her everything she wanted sexually. I pulled my manhood out of her warm, wet mouth and rubbed my head on her lips.

"Is this what you want?" I asked teasing her.

"Yes, daddy. Come get your sweetness. It's ready for you."

I could tell by her tone she was ready to burst. I got into the sixty-nine position and waited for her gushing juice of love. Within seconds she was erupting like a volcano. I took control of the dildo and turned on the vibrating feature. I placed it directly over her bulging clit. Her body shook. Regina took me into her mouth excitedly, moving rapidly up and down.

"Daddy, I need you in me. Please, daddy . . . Take it please."

I lightly blew air over her wetness, continuously teasing her, and driving her into complete frenzy of hot lustful rants.

"Daddy, fuck me. Fuck your pussy." Her hips lifted off the bed.

I had her exactly where I wanted her to be—completely under my control. I flipped over and lay on my back. I tossed the dildo to the side. "Come sit on daddy's big cock, baby. Show daddy how much you love this."

Without hesitation she jumped on top of me. I almost came after a few of her notorious hip gyrations. I loved when she was on top and arched her back exposing her firm breasts. I reached out and pulled at both her nipples. Her moans became louder. As she reached climax again, I pulled her close to me and rolled her onto her back. With ease I embraced her pink walls deeper and harder.

"Ahh, daddy, please don't stop," she whispered into my ears causing me to dig into her harsher.

"Tell me, baby. Tell daddy you'll never stay away from this again." With every word I made sure she felt what she missed.

"I'm . . . sorry, daddy. Never again, daddy. Keep fucking me, daddy. Yeah, just like that . . . ummm . . ."

I continued for the next thirty minutes, flipping her into every Kama Sutra position I knew. By the end of it all I topped her off with a mouthful of my love juice. We both plopped on the bed exhausted in every way.

"Daddy, that was so damn good . . . like you been practicing," she followed up with a laugh.

"Ahh, you got jokes, huh?" I looked to her. "I just wanted to show you what you missed. It was built up."

"Please, Tony, it's only been two days maybe three. Besides, I don't ever want you to get tired of me."

"Baby, I could never get tired of you." I pulled her into my arms and brushed her hair with my fingers. "Baby, you are the only one for me and I'm willing to wait. I'm willing to be your lover, your sex toy, your punching bag, your dick on call—"

She moved my arm and sat up. "Come on now. You know better. Maybe I should've never—"

"Don't tell me you didn't want that night to happen. Do you even remember that night? Do you remember staying on the phone for hours? Do you remember the first night we met? How our hands couldn't stay off each other so long that you rubbed on my dick under the table at the restaurant while you dined on your meal?"

"Then during dessert you slipped your fingers between my legs and made me cum. I remember." She turned to me and started to kiss my chest.

I stopped her and pulled her close to my face. "I'm willing to do anything for you. Anything." I stared into her eyes exposing my internal wish. "I want you all the time. I can't go without you now. You can't start fucking me every day for the past two months and just expect me to go cold turkey. Come on, man." I put it out there.

She smiled.

"I know for a fact that you wouldn't be fucking me if there was a choice of many. I'm not saying you wouldn't have men lined up. I'm just saying there's a reason you chose me. Am I right?" I hit her with a fact.

She squirmed a bit before she agreed with the nod of her head. "Yes, To—"

"I like it when you call me daddy."

She flickered her eyelids. "Yes, daddy, you're right in a way, but we can't get too attached. I feel you are getting attached and that's a problem."

"Attached—no, satisfied—yes, for the first time in a long time. I guess I don't want it to end. Is that so wrong?"

"No, it's not, but I don't want to be attached. I just like to fuck. Now get to it."

I laughed then pushed her down onto the bed and went to work with my lips and tongue at first. After her legs started to shake I worked my ten inches into her as I tried to remember more positions to blow her mind. *Oh, the fun I'm going to have with you!*

4

Regina

"Okay, honey, I'll see you later. Have a good day. I love you," I said to Mark before he left for work. Those words felt empty. I loved him, I truly did, but I just wasn't completely happy. I needed it all. All the money in the world wouldn't make me entirely happy, but it sure helped a lot.

The sunlight got me out of my king-sized bed. My body felt rested for the first time in weeks. I'd downsized Tony to once or twice a month. As much as I loved sex, that shit was tiring: fucking damn near every day for the past month straight for no less than two hours every session. That man put it on me like a hot curler. Every time I saw him he had me jumping at the slightest touch. He was getting too close. I was getting too close. I started to feel like an addict; I had to have it and it didn't matter where or when.

The last time I saw him was three weeks ago at China Grill in Midtown when Mark was out of town on business. I purposely set up a lunch date instead of a nightcap at a hotel. But like an addict my sobriety was tested and I failed miserably. I fucked him in the bathroom after I told him I wanted to slow things down. It was time for me to move on. It was a fling to boost my marital sex life, which it did. I may have enjoyed sex with Tony more, but mastering the moves on my man secured my future in many ways he couldn't completely fulfill.

My life was almost perfect, but there was one thing missing: a ring with meaning around my finger. Mark had provided for my every want when it came to my material and emotional demands. He only lacked in the bedroom, but it seemed that my little fling had helped me deal with his regressions in that department. I just needed that ring around my finger.

Our relationship had been eight years strong, but for the past year my feelings about that "little piece of paper" had changed. I wanted the big wedding, the engagement party, the bachelorette party, the bridal shower; I wanted it all. I was tired of being that woman who had a relationship that could be questioned because we weren't married. Everyone knew we were together and financially I was taken care like a wife. Everything had my name on it: house, summer house, cars, business, and bank accounts. I was far from stupid.

As a woman of thirty-five who couldn't have kids and didn't have a menstrual cycle every month, I might be disappointed and understandably depressed. I wasn't; not at all in the least. I found out when I was sixteen that I wouldn't have kids, my cycle wasn't normal, and it would probably just stop in my early twenties. It was actually a blessing in disguise. I was a straight slut in college, only because I couldn't get pregnant. There were too many girls who tried to keep up with me, but only became depressed by the number of abortions they had to hide from their parents. The doctors told me adopting was one of the many options for kids, but I didn't want any of that.

I hopped out the bed and headed to the kitchen. Mark was so wonderful to me; my latte was waiting on the marble countertop beside the morning paper. I took a seat on the stool and opened the paper. As I flipped through the headlines, I heard my phone sounding off. *Who the hell is calling me at this hour?* I rushed off the stool and dashed to the bedroom. By the time I got to the phone the ringing stopped. 1

Missed Call rolled across the screen. *I bet it's Tony*. I touched the screen to check the number. It wasn't Tony. It wasn't any number I knew. I looked at my phone strangely, racking my brain about the number. Suddenly, the voicemail indicator popped up. Instantly, I checked it.

"Hello, I got your number from a mutual friend, Amanda. She told me that you may be interested in my services. You can call me back at 305-678-9765, if you're still interested." His voice was raspy and borderline .

I'm going to kill this bitch Amanda for giving my personal number out! I immediately pulled up her cell number and called her.

"Hey, girl, what—"

"Who the fuck did you give my number to, bitch?" I went in on her immediately.

"Well, hey to you too. Did you even give him a chance or did you just hang up on him?"

"What? Give him a chance for what? Amanda, I'm not doing another free broker for hire. I can hear it now: 'I'm a friend of so-and-so and they said there's no fee.' I told you about that shit when you did it the first time. You better tell him to lose my number because I can't help him." I was fire hot marching back to the kitchen.

"Damn, Gina, calm the fuck down. Stop tripping."

"So tell me why you give a total fucking stranger my number?" My temper was boiling.

"Gina, he was the personal chef who catered the dinner you was so fond of last week. Remember, you asked me to pass your number along."

I felt like an ass. She was right. My hot steam defeated by a good deed.

"Why you not snapping now? Mmm-mmm. You really need to see somebody about your anger issues."

"Oh stop, okay, okay, I'm sorry. I totally forgot about that. Shit, why it took him so long to call me anyway. Wasn't he up and coming? Doesn't he need the job?"

"Please, he doesn't need anything. He's loaded with old money, girl. Cooking is just something he loves to do. And he's single. I'm trying to get him over again to cook just for me. You know, answer the door naked and see if he takes the bait. What you think?"

"Girl, do what you got to do. Are we still on for later?" She was trying so hard to get her hooks into someone; too bad she always came up with a bottom feeder.

"Oh yes, same spot at eight right?"

"Yep, I'll see you then. Sorry, again, Mandie."

"Please, bitch, I'm used to you talking out your ass." She laughed.

"Girl, you lucky I got Mark or else you would have some serious competition. Bye, bitch!" I pressed End on the screen.

Amanda was a good friend to me. I just hated lying to her. My secret had been just that: my secret. I didn't want to hear her mouth about how much I was breaking Mark's heart or how my life was too good to fuck it up like that, etc., etc., etc. My life was just that: my life. I placed my phone on the countertop and got back to checking out the headlines in the paper.

One headline after the other: nothing but immoral, foul, and heinous acts committed by man printed for everyone to read and imitate. I pushed the paper aside and gulped the last bit of my latte. I heard the front door open.

"Good morning, how are you?"

"I'm fine. How are you doing this morning, Mema?" I loved Maria. She wasn't just my housekeeper; she was my second mother. That's why I call her my Mema. I've known her since I started walking. She was my nanny as a child and when my mother died she stayed by my side as my mother would have wanted her to.

"Ahh, you know, same shit different day," she replied with her ritual answer.

"Are you still going to help me get that closet in order today?"

"Go get started. Let me do what I have to do in here."

"All right, I guess I'll go get started." She knew me so well; if I didn't start the process it would never get done.

I trotted back to my bedroom knowing that she wouldn't come in to check on me for another hour or two. My two-bedroom condo was huge compared to my tiny studio apartment by Central Park West she cleaned. Before I moved in with Mark I made it clear to him that we were a package. No matter what, Maria would be a part of our lives.

I opened the door to my walk-in closet. The scent of new leather hit my nose. There was a shopping bag with the Ferragamo logo on it by the shoe rack. "Damn him," I said with a grin. I pulled the box out the bag and opened it. "Wow, I wonder what made him pick this color." They were bright red ankle boots with a simple bow on top. It was cute, but not my color. I tossed it back in the box and put it to the side.

My walk-in closet was the size of a studio apartment. It was one of the best presents he surprised me with when he renovated. He basically kept the blueprints and contractor out of my sight while the construction was going on.

The only question he asked me was how many bedrooms I wanted. He bought the condo next door and made our already two-bedroom condo more spacious. All I did was put in my request and shop for furniture. Although I had to wait an entire year for the finished product, it was worth it.

After a year of living in a Midtown sublet, I was more than ready to move into our new space when the time came. He was very clear on me not being in the condo until it was up to my standards. Of course he hired a decorator and I didn't step foot into the place until it was perfectly in line with my taste: everything in its place; new furniture; all the things we had in storage, even my clothing, was color coordinated. It felt wonderful to step into our new home and really enjoy it, instead of unpacking.

It took us three hours to finish cleaning out my closet. I was relieved that it was all done, but the spaces on the shelves and between the hangers instantly gave me the urge to shop.

"Okay, my dear. I'm done," Maria said with exhaustion.

"Yep, I am starving." I glanced at my watch. "I better call Mark and see if he wants to catch a bite with me."

"Gina, you know good and well you should be in that kitchen cooking for that man. You really are lucky. He truly loves and adores you. But, there's a big piece missing from all this."

I knew what she was thinking: kids. After the first two years of Mark sticking around, she started to pester me about a family. Since we'd lasted so long, her pestering became a nag. I was fine without kids; besides they would only take away from *me*. My time, my money, and most of all my position in Mark's life. I rolled my eyes and tried to rush out the room before she started her lecture, rant, or guilt trip. *Let's see what it's going to be this time.*

"Where you going so fast? You know your mother would want babies, even if it's through adoption. She would want you to have a family."

There we go—the fucking guilt trip. Your mother would want this, she would want that, well, guess what, she's not here so the guilt trip won't and can't happen. When she died back then I made my decision. No kids: adoption, surrogate, or any other newfound method of having a baby.

"Come on, Mema, can we not go down that road for the hundredth time? I hate to break it to you but kids are not in my future. Maybe you can have them since you want it so bad." I got a little snappy.

"Now, Regina, you know better. All I'm saying is that maybe you could change your mind like how you suddenly want to be married. Who will you pass all this to?" She waved her arms around and followed behind me into my bedroom.

"No one. That's why I have to enjoy everything while I can. I thought you was ready to go home." I didn't hold back the hint.

"Yes, you're right. I better go." Mema walked past me with the stare of displeasure.

I hated those looks even if I deserved it. I hated to admit to myself in thought or even out loud that she was right. All the material items, first-class travel, and luxury condo on York Avenue meant nothing if you couldn't share it with a family of your own. The way I saw it the most she's going to get was a wedding.

5

Mark

I was happy to cut my day short and burn off some steam at the gym. After putting my clothes into the locker, my cell started to ring. "Hello, Mark Sands," I answered.

"Hey, baby, are you coming home soon? Can we get dinner together?" Regina responded quickly so I knew something was up.

"Do you want to go out for dinner or did you get Mema to cook again?" I chuckled. That poor woman had used every kitchen we ever owned more than Regina.

"Why you asked me like that? I thought you liked her cooking. You sure don't like mine."

Oh boy, here we go. As much as I loved this woman I only wished she would just learn how to cook. "Now you know that's not what I meant. I actually love it when you cook." I had to lie.

"Oh please, the two times I did cook I almost caught myself on fire! You're such a bad liar." Thankfully, she laughed.

"No, seriously where do you want to go? You can meet me at the gym in about an hour. I just need about forty minutes of nonstop activity. I'll see you soon." I ended the call before she could protest.

I turned my phone off and headed out the locker room toward the pool. It was still early in the day so the crowd hadn't appeared yet. As I pushed the door opened, my eyes were immediately directed to the opposite end of the pool. She stood there in a one-piece, all-white bathing suit with her blond hair hanging to her waist. There was something familiar about her as if I'd seen her before. Her tanned white skin, round, full breasts, and firm, plump ass turned me on instantly. She turned around and stared in my direction.

"You can close your mouth now," she barked showing her age.

I was completely embarrassed; grown-ass man acting like I never saw a beautiful female before when I lived with one. "Excuse me, my name is Mark Sands. You're stunning, but I'm sure you hear that all the time. I'm sorry if I made you uncomfortable." I looked around relieved to see no one in earshot.

"Are you a new member or guest?" she asked with a hint of entitlement.

No, she didn't just try to put me in my place. I was a bit offended at first, but I didn't want to show out like most young black men with money. "Actually, I've been a member for two years now. How about you?"

"Been a member for years, but rarely use my membership," she said in a much sweeter tone putting on a white robe.

"Yeah, I can understand. I didn't get your name?" I dared to ask.

"Vanessa Shore."

I did a quick "what you talkin' 'bout, Willis" face. "As in Shore & Daughters?" I shook my head knowing that it would be luck too good to have. I dropped my towel.

"As a matter of fact, yes. So I take it you heard of the company?"

"Who hasn't? You're the top builder, contractor in the city! I've been trying to pitch to your father for the past six months and I can't get a one-on-one at all."

"First, he's not my father. Six months ago we buried my father. We didn't make anything public until a month ago for legal reasons. My oldest brother runs the company now."

"I'm sorry. I didn't mean to—"

"No, no, no, it's fine. My brother is a jerk some-times, it's the Harvard mentality. Why, may I ask, would you want a one-on-one? Do you own land? Are you a subcontractor? Architect?"

She gave me that "you must need a job" or "I got this get rich quick scheme" look. "I'm a real estate broker."

"We have in-house brokers. Why should we pay a bigger percentage to a broker who doesn't hold our brand?"

I couldn't believe she was digging into me not even fully clothed. "I have a vast majority of wealthy clients and I would like the opportunity to broker your building on Greene Street, in the Village. If I can't sell out the building in thirty days, I will retire on the thirty-first day." I had to show my confident ambition.

"I see. I will have to look you up. I will have my brother call you if he's interested. If you're good, I shouldn't have a hard time getting your number." She smiled as she walked away.

"Nice to meet you, Vanessa." I lowered my voice and continued in a whisper, "Yup, it sure was nice to see you—all of you. Mmmm mmmm good." I grabbed my crotch wishing for one night alone. She was smart, young, and hot; who wouldn't want to tap that ass?

I jumped into the pool to cool off and work that lustful tension out of me with some laps.

**

Two days later I was sitting in my office when the phone rang.

"Mark Sands."

"Hello, Mark, this is Vanessa Shore."

I jumped out my seat almost dropping the phone. "Yes, yes, how are you? I see you found me just fine."

"I'm well. Actually, you have a rising reputation."

"Rising?" I didn't want to take it as an insult, but my tone showed my distaste for her so-called compliment.

"Yes, rising. I feel that all brokers who never dealt with my company are rising so don't take it personally. You must understand my company is family owned and most of our brokers we have been dealing with for decades. At one time we had a mother and daughter team. But enough of that, from the looks of it my brother wants to meet with you to discuss your proposal. How long would it take you to get to the Mercer Hotel?"

I quickly glanced at my watch: 4:30. "How about an hour?"

"Okay, we are in the penthouse suite. See you in an hour."

When I heard the final click on the phone, I screamed, "Yes!" My office was located on Madison Avenue and Fifty-seventh Street. My home was only fifteen minutes away. I knew it would be a rush but I knew I would be there in no more than an hour.

I dashed out the building and hailed a cab. "Eighty-ninth and York Avenue, please." Before I knew it we were pulling up to my building. When I looked at my watch it took the cab less than fifteen minutes. I reached into my pocket. "Damn, that was fast." I looked at the meter: $14.76. I peeled a fifty dollar bill from my money clip. "Keep the change, you deserve it. Any chance you'll be out here in twenty minutes?" I questioned stepping out the car.

"I don't know. I take a break soon."

"Okay, thanks." I closed the car door and with haste flew past the doorman with a rushed greeting through the front door toward the elevator. I entered and pushed 21 on the panel. I was nervous. This was an opportunity that would open countless doors for me in real estate. I knew Vanessa's company scouted land around the world for the past two years in Australia, Europe, Thailand, Caribbean, and Dubai.

When the elevator opened I hurried to my condo. As I entered, I started to empty my pockets in the vestibule and hurried to the master bath.

"Damn, what's your hurry?"

Regina's voice startled me. "Shit!" I jumped.

She laughed. "I should be scared. You're the one rushing in here like a madman, geez!"

I took a deep breath. "Yes, you're right. I'm sorry, honey." I started to remove my clothes and shoes then continued, "I finally got the pitch meeting for the builders on Greene Street. Only catch is the meeting is in like forty minutes at the Mercer in SoHo. That's why I was rushing in here like a madman!" I leaped onto the bed and tickled her. Her laugh was one of the only things that put me at ease. It stifled my nervousness and anxiety for the moment.

I got her to the point of nearly urinating on herself then decided to quit before I blew my ultimate chance to become a worldwide Realtor. "Okay, I'm done. I better get into the shower and get dressed. I don't want to be late."

"Yes, please go, go, please." She continued to laugh.

After I showered, then put on one of my best suits and splashed a little cologne, I was ready to conquer whatever lay before me. "Okay, babes, I'm heading out. I will call you afterward, maybe you can come meet me." I gave her a kiss on the lips and headed out the door. I glanced at my watch in the elevator: 5:10. I had twenty minutes to get there.

My nervousness was easing its way back in. *Think of your credentials, what you can bring to the table, your buyers list . . .* My bullet points were repeated in my mind as I hopped into a cab. "The Mercer in SoHo, please."

The driver was very slow going. How I wished the previous driver was in control. It was like he was purposely catching all the lights. I glanced at my watch: 5:20. I pulled out my cell, but soon realized Vanessa called me at my main office not on my cell. I started preparing my excuses for my lateness in silence. After about fifteen minutes of stop and go I finally made it. I swiped my credit card and hurried out the cab.

Before I entered the building, I adjusted my suit jacket and smoothed my hair with the palm of my hand. *All set.* I got onto the elevator staring into the brass walls fixing myself. When the doors opened I was surprised to see Vanessa standing there. I damn near barged right into her. "Oh—"

"Mark, I—"

"I'm sorry. Are you okay?"

"No, no, I'm fine. I was just heading downstairs for a moment. Just knock on the door to the right. I shouldn't be long."

"Okay, see you in a bit." I turned and walked slowly toward the door all the while thinking how weird for her to leave. Was she not a part of the business?

I knocked on the door, twice.

A tall, well-dressed, all-American white male answered the door. "Hi, you must be Mark Sands." He extended his hand.

I shook it with a strong grip. The room was actually set up really nicely. Huge living room, even a dining area; although there was a tiny kitchenette it was a well-staged apartment. "Hello, nice to meet you, Charles, right?"

"Yes, the younger one is the junior, Scott. Can I offer you anything to drink or eat?" He gestured for me to be seated.

"No, I'm fine for now."

"So, Vanessa tells me you're confident in selling out Greene Street in thirty days. All fifteen units?"

"Yes, that's why I started calling you six months ago to get this meeting." I gave a light chuckle then continued, "When will the building be done? I bet some of those permits were a bitch to get." I knew exactly when the company brought the lot.

"It should be done in about ten months."

"So, I assume you broke ground already and the iron shell is done, right? You know I'll need more than just the floor plans to sell out. My clients are well known and wealthy, but if they can't see the vision it won't happen. Right now SoHo is hot. I can get some sophisticated, young up and comers, 'new to the city' types. I mean, let's be honest, you don't want just anybody in your building. You want your buildings to be talked about, on covers of magazines, maybe even some international publicity." His brows arched so I knew his interest piqued.

"You have international clients? Have you worked abroad before?"

"I've done enough internationally to have a list." I wasn't going to just give him a slam in my face after he entered.

"Okay, let's just cut to the chase. Your name has come to my attention before, but your percentage is what turns me off. You want five percent more than other private brokers in the state. Now, my question to you is, are you worth that much?"

I heard the door open and in walked Vanessa. "I hope my brother hasn't been too rude."

"Nothing but business. As for your question, Charles, I am still the number one broker in the state and soon to be abroad. My take in for the year is nothing less than ten million. Now, you tell me what broker in your firm brings in that amount of profit?"

"Mark, the bottom line is if you can sell out Greene Street in thirty days while in construction then we can seriously talk about our future projects here and abroad."

"Okay, so this means your team of brokers will not be a part of any advertisements or contracts. Your company has solely given me thirty days to follow through with my exclusivity on the property. Agreed?" I waited intently for his response. I knew he was playing with my ego and thought maybe I might want his help. I didn't need or want it. I like to run my own show.

With a few strokes of his chin and a few "hmms" Charles agreed. "I will have my lawyer send you the contract for this deal. You have thirty days once the contract is signed."

"Okay, since business is out the way, let's get some drinks to seal the deal," Vanessa interjected preparing to raid the minibar.

"Actually, I really must go. My wife is waiting for me at home. It's date night," I lied as I fluttered my eyes. I shook Charles's hand and waved a good-bye to Vanessa then headed out the door.

As I stepped into the elevator and watched the doors close, I removed my blazer immediately feeling my perspiration through my shirt. *Yes, I did it. This is going to bring me all the way to the top,* I thought loosening my tie. I walked out the hotel with a big smile. I pulled out my cell to call Regina. One, two, three rings then straight to voicemail.

"Hey, I got the deal for Greene Street. I was hoping we could celebrate when I get home. See you soon." I hung up the phone a little disappointed that she didn't pick up, but I shrugged it off. *I guess I will see her soon enough.*

6

Vanessa

"Well, wasn't that rude," I said with much displeasure.

"Vans, I hope I won't regret this. I'm depending on you to make sure he keeps his word." Charles opened his laptop set on the desk.

He started to click away as I opened the bottle of champagne. "Do you want a glass or should I just go out on the terrace and drink by myself?" I hinted that his company was needed. I grabbed two glasses and the bottle then headed to the terrace overlooking the busy nightlife of SoHo Village.

My brother stood six foot four inches with a model body, clean-cut hair, and he worked out his muscles every day and I mean every day, even Christmas. He could have anyone he wanted, but his love life seemed uneventful through the years. We were only a year apart so our circle was mostly the same and we were extremely close. So close that sometimes our own friends and family would wonder. But there was never anything incestuous going on; I just trusted him with any- and everything. We had no secrets.

"Pour me a glass, I'll join you in a minute."

Setting the bottle on the floor, I opened the French doors and took in the night air. It wasn't too hot; the humidity had died down and the cool air from the Hudson was inviting. I picked up the bottle and walked out onto the terrace. Since we were in one of the penthouses the terrace was huge: corner to corner lined with double glass five foot wall at the edge. The patio furniture was all wrought iron with huge, plush white and orange cushions. There was a bistro table next to one of the lounge chairs. I placed the bottle on top and poured myself and my brother a glass.

"Charles, are you coming? Charles?" I knew he heard me. "Come on, stop working already."

The clicking had stopped and I could hear him approaching.

"All right, where's my glass."

I gestured to the small table beside me.

"Okay, should we toast to this deal or do you have something else in mind?"

"Now, you know I don't give two shits about that deal, as long as he gets the job done." I raised my glass and gently knocked his glass.

"Well, I guess I don't have to worry about it getting done." He raised his brow.

"What's that look about?" I sipped from my glass.

"Oh, don't think I don't know you. Why were you so eager for him to see me tonight instead of at the office? Are you thinking of fucking him?"

I rolled my eyes regretting that I even came back upstairs. I really thought Mark would hang around. When he mentioned his wife I looked at his left hand and didn't see any ring. That left me to conclude he was either in a committed relationship or just wanted us to stay out of his personal life.

"Damn, what's the deal with all the questions? Geez!"

"I know those looks." He scanned me from head to toe and gave me the "I know you" look.

"Please, you heard him, he's married." I hoped I wasn't that transparent to Mark. My brother knew me well enough to know marriage was only a temporary locked door for me. I always got whatever I wanted.

"Just make sure he does what he has to do first before you fuck up his world." He downed his drink and put his glass on the table. "I'm serious.

Listen I'm heading out, but you better think before you do. I'm not going to deal with your shit again. You'll have to clean it up yourself."

"What can I say? I'm my father's daughter in more ways than one."

His eyes told me not to, but it only made me want to even more. I brushed his comment off, telling myself that he was still mad about my last affair with a married man. I was still paying him back for all the money he had to pay out. Deep down I knew he was still angry about how our father died. It was me who caused his massive heart attack. I only wished I could turn back the clock.

"Vanessa, why are you doing this?"

"Doing what, Daddy? It's not my fault."

"You can't keep doing this. You've gone too far with this shit. You're young, you can still get yourself together."

"Why does it bother you so much? We are all consenting adults. I didn't force him to talk to me, you did that. Or do you not remember telling me to make sure I learned everything from him? I didn't hold a gun to his head. He knew exactly what he was doing."

"Fine, I understand where you're coming from, but you're screwing with this man's family. His life. Our lives. Do you know your mother can't

look in your direction anymore? Why do you think she left on a two month vacation? I can't. I just can't anymore." He took a seat in his chair and clutched his glass holding his favorite Scotch. He brought the glass to his lips and took a gulp. His face looked flushed.

"It doesn't matter anyway, he's leaving his wife. I'm only following your footsteps. Have you had your weekly late-night dinner meeting yet?"

My dad's mouth dropped open. I hated that he always had to control everything: the way I acted, where I lived, who I dated, where I went to school, who my friends were. Enough was enough. I was tired of being controlled and groomed into a person I had no interest in being. I was furious at him for talking to me as a child without sense.

"How . . . Where . . . Did your mother tell you that?" He was shocked that I knew about his adulterous affair.

"Do you hear yourself? You're such a hypocrite! Tell me, you can be honest with me."

"I don't know what you're talking about, but I can't have you ruin someone else's life again." His voice was getting louder.

"I don't want him. I've already moved on with his son." I stormed out not looking back,

knowing my revelation would undoubtedly cause some hardship to swallow.

"Va-ness-a-a . . ."

I heard his short breaths and he tried to shout my name, but I didn't bother to turn around. Instead I headed out to the front door. Charlie was pulling into the driveway as I rushed into my car. I waved to him and sped off.

An hour later I received a phone call from Charlie screaming at me to get to the hospital. He didn't say anything over the phone but the address of the hospital then just hung up. When I tried calling him right back he never picked up. I called every one of my other siblings and still no one picked up. I was scared. I was at least an hour away from Lenox Hill Hospital. I sent a group text to all of my brothers and sisters: I wish one of you would pick up your fucking phone. I can't get there for another hour. Now some one better tell me what the FUCK is going on!

I was entering Park Slope, Brooklyn off the BQE. I didn't know what was going on. I immediately jumped back on to the highway and headed toward the hospital dipping and dodging out of lanes. I was surprised I didn't get pulled over.

Finally, I arrived at the hospital to see my younger brother outside smoking a cigarette. I rushed to him. "Brent, what the fuck is going on?" His eyes were red like he was crying. Brent's hand was shaking as he put the cancer stick to his lips. I grabbed his shoulders and demanded to know why I was called here.

"He's dead. Our father died of a heart attack over an hour ago. Charlie found him on the floor in the den. He tried to do CPR and shoved an aspirin down his throat, but by the time the ambulance got him here it was too late. The doctors did all they could." He was trying to hold back his tears.

My heart sank and my knees started to buckle. My eyes flooded with water. I couldn't believe it; my very last words to him was nothing but selfish and out of anger. I didn't want to believe him. I slid down to the ground clutching my chest hoping I would wake up soon.

"Vans, do you want to go say good-bye? Everybody is upstairs except for Mom. She can't get a flight until the morning." He wiped his red eyes with the bottom of his T-shirt and plucked his cigarette into the street.

I sat there stunned staring out at nothing. His voice sounded like it was far away, not real, until he reached down and shook my shoulder. I screamed, "No, this is a dream. I'm going to wake up. I'm going to see Dad."

Brent tried to stop me from jumping into a cab, but I dipped and dodged his reaches. When I got into the cab I shouted the address and the urgency of time. I sat back watching the people move by. After twenty minutes of being in a trance-like state, the cab stopped in front of my parents' home in Queens. I reached into my purse and just handed him a fifty dollar bill; I didn't bother to look at the fare flashing in red.

Was it true? My dad's car was still in the driveway alongside my mom's. I rushed to the door and rang the doorbell erratically. There was no answer. I knew where the spare key was. I walked around to the back of the house, opened the gate, and picked up the fake rock on the ground. I opened the rock and pulled the key out recklessly almost dropping it o the ground. I ran back to the front door. My hands were shaking, the key jiggling as I tried fitting it into the keyhole. It took a minute, but I finally got the key in and unlocked the door. I was such in a rush I left the key in the keyhole as I dashed into the house running toward my dad's den. I was shouting, "Dad, Dad, where are you?"

The glass on the floor and the smell of liquor hit me. "Oh my God! No, no . . . No." I fell to the floor screaming.

I remembered like it was yesterday. I knew Charlie still resented me for catapulting him to his death. It was never spoken, but if I'd stayed there he may have lived.

I continued to sip on my champagne and let the night sky float by. I only wished Mark stayed so I could get to know him a little better. *I guess I will have to do it on my own.*

7

Regina

It was still early and I didn't want to go to dinner with Mark so I ignored his call. I sent a text instead: Mandie just called. Am going out with her. Don't wait up. Hope your meeting went well. Honestly, I was ready to go have some fun without him. He was so predictable. First dinner with a bottle of wine then go home to have robot sex like an old married couple. I was seriously tired of that. It would be a different story if we were married; then I would learn to live with it.

I grabbed my Chanel purse and walked out the door, praying that I wouldn't bump into Mark on the way out. I dialed Amanda immediately.

"Hey, girl, how you doing?" I greeted her.

"I'm good, what's going on with you?"

"Girl, I just got into a huge fight with Mark. I'm going to a hotel for the night."

"Are you serious? Was it that bad?" Amanda asked sounding concerned.

"No, it really wasn't. I'm just punishing him. I just wanted to make sure you don't take his call when he calls you. You know, to find out where I am." I lied, but I knew she would fall for it. She's so gullible. I was grinning ear to ear just thinking about it.

"Okay, no problem. I got your back. You sure you just don't want to come over here? It's not like I got a man over here or anything. Why pay all that money for a hotel?"

"Thanks, girl, but I think I need to digest what he just said to me. I can't talk about it right now because I'll just burst into tears again." I gave a slight sniffle then continued, "Besides, I'm not paying for it. I took his credit card."

"I know that's right. Well, when you ready to talk I'm always here for you. At least tell me which hotel you going to, girl."

I hesitated for a moment. "Umm, hmmm . . . Maybe the Hilton in Midtown or the penthouse suite at the Mercer. That will show him."

"Make sure you remove every bottle from the minibar. That should add more to the heavy bill you plan on making."

I laughed. "You got that right. He's lucky he doesn't have a black Amex yet. Or else it would have been on a private jet to Dubai for a week."

We both laughed.

"Definitely. Well, when you do don't forget about your dear old friend over here. I may find my husband there." She continued to laugh.

"Okay, girl, I just wanted to give you the heads-up."

"Oh, don't worry. After I hang up, my phone will be off until the morning. I'll talk to you tomorrow."

"Thanks, talk to you later." I smiled at the thought of having a night all to myself to have some fun.

I pushed End on my phone and slid it into my purse. For damn sure someone was going to see me in this dress. I giggled at the thought. I always felt unstoppable when I was dressed to kill. My tight, bright summer teal dress with gold embellishments lining my plunging neckline hit its mark. My hair was swept into a sexy bun to direct more attention toward my girls up top. And my Jimmy's were on point matching the gold tone of the embellishments. The night air guided me downtown on the Lower East Side to meet up with Tony. He mentioned something about introducing me to some friends.

It wasn't that I didn't want to see him; I was just tired of him. He was becoming predictable like Mark. Definitely something I did not want.

When I decided to slow it down with Tony I was clear that he couldn't call me. He would have to wait for my call and Tony came running every time I did. I only kept him at arm's reach because I didn't know if I could find the same secrecy Tony had shown me in someone new. But now that I'd seen all his tricks, there was nothing willing me to keep his ass around. He was aware leaving Mark for him was not in the future.

When the cab pulled up to the address, I immediately pulled out my phone to double check the address Tony texted me earlier. My hesitation showed on my face.

"Are you sure this is the correct address, miss? This doesn't look like your type of crowd."

The driver was right. The building had broken bricks layered at the top, drunk old men sitting at a makeshift table playing dominoes, women scattered about as if they were waiting for someone to pick them up. I looked at my phone again. *This is the right address, but this can't be it,* I thought. I looked to the driver. "Would you mind just waiting a few so I can get a hold of my friend? You can leave the meter running."

"Sure, no problem," the driver answered.

I texted Tony immediately: I'm here. Come outside or I leave in 5.

I waited for what seemed like minutes, but within seconds of pressing the Send button Tony appeared in front walking toward the cab.

"Okay, I guess the address was right. That will be $23.40."

I handed him thirty dollars and told him to keep the change. I stepped out the cab feeling uneasy. "Tony, I thought this was a socialite event. This doesn't look right." I stopped.

He took me in his arms. "Trust me, Regina. It's something right up your alley. After tonight you may just finally leave that square of a man you're with." He smiled and pecked my lips.

His words still weren't reassuring me, but his smooth voice and strong arms felt safe enough. I pulled him closer and pressed my soft lips against his. His tongue slid into my mouth pushing his warm, minty taste forward.

"Hmm, you taste so good. Let's go in. I promise you will love it."

"Okay, but if it's not up to my standards, Tony, you're putting me in a cab." I held on to his arm as we walked past the riffraff.

We approached a heavy black metal door and opened it. It felt as if I stepped into a black box. I couldn't see a thing. I clutched Tony's hand harder. My heart started to pump.

Suddenly a deep voice asked, "Name?"

I screamed silently while squeezing Tony's hand even more. It sounded as if he was directly behind me. His hot breath hit the back of my ear. "Red Velvet," Tony answered.

Red velvet, what the hell is that? I thought. I still couldn't see anything. The suspense was killing me. Whose party was this?

A red light turned on, and a door was opened. The smell was intoxicating. I felt like I was in another world. We were met at the door by a tall woman dressed in an all-black lace lingerie ensemble: thigh-high netted stockings, bustier fitted like a glove, no panties; and her breasts were perfectly perched for admiring. She held two masquerade masks in her hand, both red.

"Welcome to our intimate red velvet event. Please put the mask on."

I was intrigued. From what I could see, everyone had a mask on just different colors. There were only a few couples talking and sipping on their drinks, all dressed very nicely nothing like the hostess who greeted us. It didn't look like a party at all. I wanted to ask Tony what kind of party this was, but I thought I already knew. The room we entered was draped in red: red lighting, red roses everywhere, red comfy lounge chairs dead center of the room, and a small side bar off toward the rear of the room.

It seemed like a warehouse and pretty empty for a party. We put on the masks and were ushered to a lounge chair.

"Your hostess will greet you in a minute. She will go through the rules and take your drink orders. Have a wonderful time." She left us, swaying her nicely shaped butt out the room.

I tried to listen to any one of the couples in earshot as we were waiting, but my excitement wouldn't let me. "Tony, is this some kind of sex party?" I flashed a wicked smile.

"I thought maybe you needed something new. Are you okay with that?"

Of course I was okay with that. I was surprised, but didn't think to show him my gratitude just yet. I'd been secretly looking for something like this, but would never admit it to Tony. "We'll see."

Just then, a fully clothed woman approached us with a warm smile and more masks in different colors. "Hello, you must be Mr. and Mrs. Smith, my pleasure to meet you." She extended her hand to me first then Tony.

"Nice to meet you," Tony replied.

"Well, let's get started. First, you both are wearing red masks indicating this is your first event with us as a couple. You have the opportunity to continue as a couple or as individuals. I have a few colors here: yellow, green, black, or white. Yellow for those exploring as individuals, green for those who want to try new things, black for those who are more aggressive in their passion, and finally white for those who just want to watch only. You can always keep the red masks on and move as a couple throughout the venue. There are some rules. First no drugs; if you are caught with any you will immediately be escorted out and your credit card on file will be charged a five thousand dollar fine. You will also be blacklisted from any future events in this society. If you have anything on you I can take the contraband now and you will be able to proceed without any infractions." She smiled, and looked to Tony.

"No need for it," Tony responded.

"Great. Second, there is a safe word to stop any situation you are uncomfortable in. The safe word is 'elephant.' There is a security guard in every room. Third, if you move as a couple, you stay as a couple. Meaning, that any activity you participate in your partner must be present and involved whether it's contributing or watching. Your partner must be present in the same room. When you go through those doors"—she pointed to a large solid oak door across the room—"there are different rooms you can enter and interact with others. Every person here has been screened. There are condoms in every room or lounge area. We leave it up to the individual or couple to practice safe sex. Lastly, I will have to take any electronic devices on you along with your purse and wallet for security reasons. You will place them into a locked security box where only you can open it. All security boxes are placed into a guarded room where entry can only be made with a key card held by me only. Now that we got that out the way, what can I get you to drink?"

"We'll take two glasses of Patrón with ice and salted lime wedges."

"Okay, I'll be back with your drinks and the lockbox for your belongings. Don't forget to choose a color to continue with." She set the platter of masks on a small table beside us and walked over to the bar. A huge six foot shadow suddenly appeared following her.

"Wow, this is . . ." I didn't want to react. My insides were flipping around, in a good way. But if I'd shown him how anxious I was he would have seen an opportunity to get back in. I didn't want it to go there. I had him at my beck and call, not me at his.

"This is your chance to back out now if it's something you don't want to do. I don't want

you to feel pressured just because we're here."
He picked up the green mask.

"Green, you want to try something new?"

"Isn't that the reason we're here? If it's not our
tea we can always leave."

"Well, there's the safe word." He passed me a
green mask, but I pushed his hand away. "Maybe
next time."

The hostess returned with our drinks in hand
and the lockbox carried by her six foot shadow.
He was definitely intimidating with his broad
shoulders, big chest, at least 300 pounds, arms
as big as thighs; and the lighting made him just
plain ol' scary.

"Okay, here we go. Your drinks." She placed
each glass into our hands. "Have you decided
on your color for the night?" She looked to her
shadow and took the lockbox and placed it in
front of us. He then handed her a tablet. She
swiped on the screen and presented it to us.
"Can both of you place your right thumbs on the
screen for a few seconds. This way you can open
the lockbox."

We did as she asked. I was impressed. These
parties must bring in an exclusive crowd. The
security seemed topnotch. She then requested
us to place our thumbs on a black screen on
top of the lockbox. Two seconds later the door

popped opened. I handed Tony my purse and he put it in along with his cell phone and money clip.

"Please close the door. Thank you." She handed the box to her shadow. "The box cannot be opened without your thumbprints. Now have you decided on your color?"

"Yes, red."

"Okay then, Mr. and Mrs. Smith, you can proceed through those double doors and enjoy your night." She picked up the tray of masks and walked away with her shadow following.

"Okay, you ready to explore? From what I heard we should have lots of fun." He grabbed my hand and led me through the double doors.

With drinks in hand we stepped through the doors. The lights were very dim staying with the same red color. There were daybeds scattered throughout. It was a very large warehouse separated into different sections by hanging sheer curtains. All types of moans and groans could be heard: some cursing in ecstasy, some reaching their climax, and some encouraging others to go harder.

It was overwhelming at first to see all those naked bodies scattered about going at it. But after a few minutes and a few sips of Patrón along with Tony's hand wrapped around my body those nerves subsided. We walked around the large space slowly, taking notes on how everyone was interacting with each other. One scene had at least four voyeurs watching while pleasing themselves, nude bodies with green and red masks on were layered on top of each other licking, inserting, and rubbing all over each other. It was like a live porno play.

Scantily dressed women and men were walking around with serving trays displaying condoms, lubrication, whips, handcuffs, blindfolds, and even vibrators. I noticed that servers were picking up clothes as they hit the floor and slipping bracelets on to their wrists. It was done very smoothly without disturbing the mood of the situation. It was an upscale swinger's party. I was so amazed at how free everyone was. There were men on men, women on men, women on women; it was a secret dream come true. On the inside I wanted to strip bare and join the closest group next to me. We continued to another scene.

"Tony, this is—"

"Just what you wanted." He smiled.

I think my grin was bigger than his. "Let me find out that you're finally over the fact that you can't have me all to yourself. But you've been keeping all this a secret, why?" I waved my hand then took another sip of my drink.

"You wouldn't believe me if I told you."

"Oh yeah, like you haven't been to one of these before." I rolled my eyes and looked away. I wasn't mad, but getting rid of him for good would be senseless.

"Honestly, I'd never been. I only got an invite because I used one of my boys' name."

"And who is your boy?"

"You will never meet him. Remember our agreement: there are no meet-and-greets with anyone in our personal lives." He gave me a little wink and nod then emptied his glass. As one of the servers walked by he placed the glass on the tray.

I was ready to get it started. My skin was hot, and my arousal started to bubble over. I watched Tony undress, so I followed suit. I placed my empty glass on a tray as a server slipped my bracelet on to my wrist. I kept my shoes on, only because I didn't want them to be mishandled or someone thinking it's okay to try them on.

"Do you want—"

Before he could finish his question my feet led me away. I spotted a chiseled chest, defined abs, strong arms, and a well-endowed white man, which was rare from what I'd been told. When I was in college I dated a few white guys, but they always fell short so I never got that point. My hot spot was already overflowing watching him dig deep into this woman while another was shoving her tongue down his throat. I didn't care to look if Tony was behind me or not. *I am getting a taste of that,* I thought.

I eased closer, staring at him. He had a green mask on, which meant he wanted something new. My mind was set on showing him something new. I stood there with my nipples erect, my clit throbbing, and ready for him to slam his ten wide inches into me. I suddenly felt Tony's readiness to bend me over and do me right there, but I wasn't having it. I placed myself at the edge of the daybed like a begging dog. He stopped momentarily, and reached for my right breast. I let out a soft moan welcoming his touch.

"I've never had chocolate before. Can only you join?"

"Let me show you what a little bit of chocolate can do for you." I licked my lips and lifted a fresh condom of the tray next to the bed. "Let's just make it clear: you can't stick me and anyone else at the same time." I handed him the condom.

He moved of the bed and removed the rubber from his penis and placed the new one on. I heard the female, who was on all fours, on the bed groaning for more. I smiled watching the other woman slowly move off the bed.

"You ladies have had me long enough. It's time for something new," he said to the ladies, then looked to me.

That was my cue. I grabbed his stiff manhood and gently stroked while nudging him to lie on the bed. "Are you ready?" I playfully said as I licked the tip of his dick. "Mmm, bubblegum, my favorite." He felt so good in my mouth. I couldn't help myself as I eased his entire shaft into my mouth; he was a perfect fit. I went slowly up and down, loving every minute of it. Tony was far from my mind. I was sure he stood there and watched. I was too involved to care. I took my time making him moan and squirm.

"Please let me taste you," he whined.

For some reason I didn't and wouldn't stop. I just started moving my hand in a twisting motion quickly with my mouth securing his cock. He seemed to like it even more, which made me drip more and more. Suddenly, I felt a hand rubbing my ass cheek. It made me stop to look back. It made my moaning partner sit up too.

"Hey, buddy, she's partying alone in this scene."

"What? Do you not see that we're a couple?"

Everything stopped. I was embarrassed, mortified, that Tony would actually make a scene at a place like this. I even saw security moving closer. Everyone was standing around waiting for shit to hit the fan.

"Tony, stop acting like a possessive fool and go have some fun elsewhere," I muttered under my breath. I then turned to my naked companion. "Don't worry he's not joining." As soon as I said that, I saw security approaching.

Security was all in black, two stocky males, at least 275 pounds and over six feet tall, reaching for Tony. I didn't want to be humiliated even more so I quickly got off the bed and got in between security and Tony. At that point all eyes were on us.

"Tony, please." I felt the heat rise in my cheeks.

"Excuse me, miss, is there a problem?" one male security sternly asked, ready to toss Tony to the side.

"No, not at all," Tony answered.

"Miss, as policy if your husband or boyfriend does not agree with your actions, both of you will be asked to exit."

I was all set to go off on Tony, but I chose to put Tony at ease. "There's no problem." I quickly removed myself from the bed.

"That sucks," I heard from my naked acquaintance.

"Sorry, maybe next time." I brushed through Tony and security. I was ready to leave.

"Regina, wait," I heard Tony calling.

His possessiveness was showing its ugly head again. We spoke on this once before. I even cut his ass off for a while and now that he finally stepped it up, I was forced to kick him to the curb like an old pair of shoes. I tapped on the arm of the first server I saw. "Excuse me, can you get me my things?" I tried to be casual as possible, not to expose my ignominy. I walked over to one of the empty lounge chairs against the wall and took a seat. I looked around at the world I was just teased with, wishing that my unfortunate incident didn't cause anything but a minor fee and not lifetime ban.

I could see Tony walking toward me. *Oh hell, if he starts some shit, I'm calling security my damn self,* I thought.

"Regina, I thought you wanted to experience this as a couple. If you want to we can change our masks. I don't care who you fuck, suck, lick, or pour yourself over. I brought you here to show you I'm not jealous. I don't care if I have to share you, besides aren't you moving on? Getting married?"

He pitched my lie directly to my face without a blink. Tony's voice was extremely calm even when the server came by with my clothes, not skipping a beat when he passed her his bracelet for his items. My shock kept me silent. I didn't want to cause any more of a scene so I just slid my dress on in a hurry.

"Okay, so I guess you want to leave."

"Yeah." My voice cracked a bit. "Umm, I don't think I was ready for it . . . with you . . . anyway." I heard his chuckle behind me. Oh, how I wanted to slap the shit out of him.

"You right."

I felt the enormous grin he must have had plastered across his face. Suddenly I remembered, *I can't get that lockbox open without him. Shit!* My rushed pace suddenly slowed. I turned around and he was wrestling with gravity to put his clothes on. I died of laughter on the inside. He wasn't getting that satisfaction; instead I got madder. I stood there with my arms folded across my chest looking at my wrist as if I was wearing a watch. I was only less than fifty steps from the huge double doors to exit.

"Just a minute." He realized I was waiting instead of bucking through the doors, so he got a hold of himself and got dressed.

"I can't get my shit without you or did you forget about that?" I belted at him when he walked over.

"No, but it seemed you just grasped the situation by the way you stood still in slow motion," he snapped back.

"Please, it seems like you forgot who I am."

"You can't be anything more than what you portray yourself to be." He was digging into me deep.

I pushed the door open. *Ooh, you motherfucker, I'm going to make you pay for that little comment,* my mind chimed. I walked over to one of the lounge chairs and took a seat breathing very slowly to calm myself. What felt like minutes was truly seconds before a provocatively dressed waitress approached us.

"Can I help you?"

"Yes, we would like our things," Tony stated.

"Of course, your hostess will be with you momentarily. Can I get you something to drink before you go?"

"No, thanks," I thoughtfully said with a smile. I wanted to come back to the same welcoming service. She walked away talking into her headset.

After a few minutes of sitting in silence, the hostess approached. "Is everything all right?"

I stood up. "Yes, it's just my date had another idea in mind." I raised my brows and leaned in closer to her. "I think he forgot what I paid for."

The hostess did nothing but smile at my comment then looked to Tony. I hoped he felt like shit! The hostess kindly presented us with the tablet cued for us to place our thumbs on. The security placed the lockbox on the small table beside the lounge chair. It took only seconds before the lockbox opened. As soon as I retrieved my purse, I stood up and looked to the hostess. "Thank you. Is there a card I can get to be invited again?"

"We don't have cards. Everything is done by referral. As you know this is a very exclusive club and to be invited you will need a referral."

I was confused. *Is Tony a member?* "Can you tell me who referred us?"

"You were a guest of your date, Tony. He has been a member for about a year. He can send me the referral with your e-mail address without a problem."

My face was probably red. "Okay." I looked to Tony. "Can you send her the referral now please?" He looked surprised.

"I can do it that later," he snapped.

The hostess took her cue and left us immediately. I was pissed. This type of event was all I needed. I wouldn't need Tony to satisfy me; I would have my choice. I needed that referral and I was going to make sure I got it.

"Okay, Tony, you made your point. Now can we just go to the hotel so you can get what you really wanted instead all of this?" I waved my hand around.

"Oh, so that's it, huh? It's me, huh?" He smiled and chuckled a bit.

I put on my best puppy-dog, "have sympathy for me" look. "I'm sorry, daddy. Do you forgive me?"

Of course he would forgive me. He said it himself: I was the one.

8

Mark

I thought having dinner together would be nice, but I guess takeout it will be. Lately, Regina had been distant. She spent more and more time away from me. Even when I was around she found an excuse to leave me. I didn't know how to ask why she was avoiding me or more honestly I didn't want to ask her. I knew why: the ring.

All the magazines, articles, books layered throughout the condo about the perfect marriage, the most exotic wedding location, the who's and what's of proper wedding etiquette, and of course the thick, heavyweight *Wedding Planning for Dummies*. I hated the idea of a *wedding:* the stress of who to invite, the money wasted on the venue for only a few hours, the amount of crappy-ass gifts you'll return, and of course the plus-ones you will never encounter again. It all seemed so mediocre and not to mention an expensive, lavish party to show your guests just how much you love your significant other.

It was simple to me really: find a mate who you can live with and build a life together without the legal binding hold of a marriage. What if after four years your relationship changes for the worse, then what? How do you go through the humiliating fact you couldn't keep the marriage afloat? Then, as if dealing with that wasn't enough, you're forced to put a value on all the years you were married.

I thought attaching Regina to my bank accounts and properties she would be happy because in the end that's what it all comes to: money. I wasn't an idiot about it; my accountant made sure a hefty stipend of funds was deposited into my offshore accounts on the other side of the globe. Regina only had knowledge of my worth from the information I provided. I allowed her to have full control of the properties we owned. I thought by giving her an executive title and free rein on all decisions she would be satisfied, thinking she would be content in running her own company and making her own money. I still took care of all the bills and provided for her as any husband or man should so the cold shoulder and dismissive behavior didn't come from money.

It seemed as if "the ring" was now becoming more and more shoved in my face. She always knew I never believed in "marriage." I believed in love and no paper or party could ever show that. Marriage was a piece of paper that could be shredded in seventy-two different ways or retracted in hours. There was no doubt about my love for her, but I wanted kids and she couldn't reproduce. Adopting wasn't the same. I needed my blood, my DNA, running through my kid's veins. I didn't want a piece of paper defining who *my* kids were or were going to be. If I wanted a family with this woman I would have to accept adoption or create my child in a petri dish.

I sat there staring out the window contemplating my future with the one woman I would die for and the many women I would have to go through to find love again. There was only one thing to do: accept the unacceptable and do the unthinkable. "I will marry her," I confirmed out loud. It took a lot to say those words, but if it would make her happy then I'd do it. *What could go wrong? I've been with her long enough. There shouldn't be any surprises.* I grabbed my phone and scrolled to my calendar. Buy ring, I typed in.

I looked at the time on my watch: 7:00 p.m. *Damn, it's still early. I can't call her now,* my mind told me. Disturbing her fun would be selfish of me. Instead I finished my Thai dinner and headed to bed. I had to be well rested before the nonstop madness of selling out an entire building in thirty days.

It was six o'clock the next morning and I woke up alone. *Where the hell is Regina?* I questioned myself. I called her name: "Regina. Regina." There was no response. I sat up in the bed and reached for my phone off the nightstand. I checked for any missed calls, voicemails—nothing. Usually, if she was staying out she would at least text me. I dialed her immediately. The phone just kept ringing then her voicemail picked up: "You've reached me, now leave a message." I refused to leave a message. A strange chill tickled my body. I dialed her again.

"Argh, hello." Her voice was groggy.

"Hey, baby, where are you? I woke up and you weren't here." I was concerned.

"I'm at Mandie's. We had a late night so I just slept over. What time is it?"

"It's a little after six. Will you be home soon? I need to talk to you."

"Yeah, okay. Is everything okay?" By the sound of her voice I could tell she was clueless about her actions toward me in the past days.

"Yeah, just come home soon. A lot of things are about to change and you play a huge part. Love you, see you in a bit." I waited for her to reciprocate then pushed End on the phone.

I didn't know why, but her voice was strange. I didn't know if she was still in one of her moods or what, but what I had to tell her would undoubtedly adjust it. I got out of bed rubbing the cold out my eyes and stretching toward the ceiling. I walked to the bathroom to relieve myself then headed toward the kitchen to put the coffee machine on.

I have to get the ring, and I know she probably already got one picked out. I'll check with our jeweler first. This contract has to be signed before I put anything into motion. I have to start looking at houses. We can't live in the city if we're married. I want kids and she will have to allow me that if I'm conforming to her wishes. We'll use a surrogate. Suddenly I heard my phone ringing from the bedroom. *Who the hell could that be at this hour?* I dashed to the bedroom and picked up just in time. "Mark Sands."

"Good morning, Mark, it's Vanessa. I wanted to ask you to breakfast at Norma's in the Le Parker Meridien at eight? I didn't know if you had other plans, that's why I'm calling this early."

"Only if you have the signed contract with you." I was firm. She knew her brother had the contract for more than a week now. If they were serious about selling an entire building they should've signed the contract the day it was received.

"Well, that's what I wanted to talk to you about. There were a few hiccups in there that we weren't expecting."

"I see. I've used those contracts for the past ten years. I've never had an issue with any other builder," I replied.

"So guess I'll see you at eight to work it out."

"As long as you can be held accountable when the contract is signed." I may have been a morsel too confident, but I needed this to expand to a global effect and if I had to bend I would.

"See you at eight then." The call disconnected.

I placed my phone on the counter and reached for a mug off the shelf above the coffee machine. After pouring some coffee I headed back toward the bedroom and turned on the TV. As the *Today Show* rambled off the morning's headlines I walked toward my closet to pull out one of my custom suits made by William Fioravanti over on Fifty-seventh Street. I decided on a light blue tie and my dark brown Ferragamo Oxfords. *Yes, that should make a statement,* I thought heading out the closet.

I sat on the bed to finish up my coffee and watched the *Today Show*'s newscast. I thought I heard the door open. "Regina, is that you?" There was no reply, so I headed out the bedroom. "Regina?" When I got to the front door, it was shut with no one in sight.

I didn't know if I was more disappointed in no one entering or that I was left alone for the past twenty-fours. I walked toward the kitchen and picked up my phone.

"Hello, Amanda. Sorry if I woke you, but I may need your help today."

"My help? If you're looking for Regina I can't help you," she replied with an attitude as if I was the worst person in the world.

"Damn, what did I do now?"

"Why don't you ask her? I don't understand how you don't know what you did. Try acting like the man she wants instead of the man who's causing her to spend a night at a hotel because of a fight you initiated."

I was confused. I thought Regina was spending the night with her. I got serious. "Amanda, what are you talking about? Wasn't Regina with you last night?"

"Ummm, listen you need to talk to Regina. I'm letting you know, as a dear friend, whatever it is that you guys are fighting about it's going to make you lose her. She told me not to take your call, but I think you need to know you are about to lose the love of your life."

I kept quiet.

"What did you do this time? How many nights is she going to spend in a hotel? Do you even care?" By her questions, I could tell she had her Nancy Grace hat on.

I almost dropped the phone. I didn't want to believe what she was asking. *Am I that blind to her goings and comings?* I questioned myself.

"Mark? Mark, are you even listening to me?"

"Actually, Amanda, I have no clue what the hell you're talking about. I have one question for you: was Regina at your house or not last night into this morning?" I felt my pulse accelerate. My mind started to race. *I've been with her so long. How could I not see this? I thought it was about the ring. What the fuck is really going on?*

"Ummm, I can't say yes or no. I ca—"

"Amanda." My voice became louder. "Amanda, you are not in a courtroom so stop covering your ass. Don't forget who got you in that law firm.

I've known you longer than Regina. If it weren't for me your ass would still be living in East New York and paying MTA like a car note. The least you can do is show me some loyalty." By her throat clearing and stumbling with words I knew there was definitely something she was keeping from me. I chimed in on her again: "Well, is there something I'm missing, Amanda?"

"I . . . I . . . I'm sorry, Mark. I—"

"If you can't be truthful about one simple question, then I just may want to come clean about everything." After I said that I knew she would have to give up whatever Regina was hiding.

A long time ago we had a chance encounter while I and Regina were going through a rough spill. She was drunk and horny and I was in a bitter revenge mode. At the time she and Regina hadn't even met yet. It was all coincidental that they ever met. Just so happened that we all ended up at the same client's party only one week after Amanda and I were intimate. She was the only other woman I really cheated with. I was a big flirt, but never went any further than words and smiles. When I bumped into her at the party it was a huge surprise and secretly written on my face that I didn't want our association known.

"Damn, that's a low blow. First, I don't want you destroying the one real friendship I have. Second, how long are you going to hold that shit over my head?"

"Hold what? The fact that I was the one who helped you change your life so that you could get out of the ghetto and receive some respect for the lawyer you are, or that you fucked your best friend's man? If I didn't know any better I would think you befriended Regina more just to get closer to me. Am I right?"

She screamed while I laughed. She was angry and boiling over like a teapot. It was funny to me how women would act. Or should I say certain women. Every moment Amanda had she did her very best to offer her goods. After many attempts she got the hint that when I was around she wasn't. The only time we were in the same room together was in public.

Amanda's reply told me she wasn't willing to let our little secret out. "I don't know what she's doing. And no, she didn't stay over here last night."

Just then I heard the front door open. I didn't hang up. As I stood there waiting I glanced at the digital clock on the microwave: 7:06. I saw Regina approaching and smiled. I returned to my conversation with Amanda. "Listen, I think we should meet for lunch to discuss everything. Do you think you can fit me in?"

"Yeah, but it'll have to be near the courthouse. I have to be able to get to court in a hurry. I'm waiting on a verdict."

"Sounds good." I pushed End on the screen and turned my attention to Regina. I pulled her close to me and gave her a peck on the lips. I wanted to get a good whiff of her scent hoping I would detect some hint of betrayal, but there wasn't. The scent of honey was all I got.

"Hey, what's going on? What do we need to talk about?" She was antsy waiting for my reply.

"I can't talk right now. I have a very important meeting at eight. It's already after seven and I still haven't showered yet. You look tired. I hope you didn't have an all-nighter at some club." I kissed her forehead and headed to the bathroom. I left her standing there confused and probably mad, but I didn't care. My entire future just changed in a blink of an eye.

9

Amanda

Oh my God, what did I just do? He wouldn't tell her or at least I hoped he wouldn't tell her. There was only one solution: beat him at his own shit. I was ready for anything and knew how to play this game very well. He forgot where I was from. Mark may have pushed me out of my comfort zone, but I wasn't about to let anything hang over my head. I grabbed my phone, swiped the screen to open a new text message.

Gina u have to call me.

I remembered that night like it was yesterday. Did he forget how he wanted it just as much as I did?

"Mark, I think you had enough to drink. I'm not about to let you go home now."

"Please, I'm fine. Just call me a cab." Mark slurred his words.

"Do you know how you look right now?"

He stood up and brushed his hand across his shoulder. "I look just fine and you can't stop me. You don't need to call a cab. I'll just go out and get one."

I jumped to my feet and got between him and the front door. "Mark, you can't go out like this. You'll probably get robbed or killed. Remember where you are?"

"I'm here with you and you're kicking me out!"

"Mark, I'm not kicking you out. You're the one who wanted to come all the way out here. I told you I would come to you. Mark, what do you really want?" His eyes told me everything.

From the first day I met Mark, I wanted him. Tonight was the first time he'd ever mentioned a woman in his life and by the looks of it she didn't know what she was losing. Mark was on the rise as one of the top Realtors in New York. What woman wouldn't stick to him like glue? Well, if she doesn't want him I will be happy to have her seconds, I thought.

I gently pecked at his soft lips as a test. I only hoped he wasn't too drunk to forget me in a few hours. He didn't resist physically, but his mind wasn't having it.

"Amanda, what are you doing? You know I'm taken. This isn't right, but I sure as hell want to fuck you."

With those words he undressed me slowly. I kissed him again and in return his manhood arose. I slid my hand over the front of his pants.

"This isn't right. I love my girl."

"Well, by the way your dick feels I don't think it matters." I unbuckled his pants and let them drop. His stiff penis easily showed through the slit in his boxers. I wrapped my hand around his shaft with my knees slightly bent and look up to him. His eyes were closed and it seemed that he was enjoying his retaliation against his girl.

"Yes. Show me . . . There's no turning back now," he whispered facing the ceiling.

I licked my lips and took him into my warm, wet mouth deeply. He moaned and pushed on the back of my head almost making me gag. After a few strokes he pulled me up and stepped out of his pants then pulled his boxers off.

"Bend over. I don't want to see your face."

After those words, my emotions took a turn. "What?" Before I could step back he turned me around and bent me over. I struggled a bit to make it rougher. Little did he know I liked playing the submissive type. Meeting a man *who liked to take control was exactly what I was looking for.*

Mark jammed his raw six inches into me. I received him like a linebacker, pushing every time he pumped into me. Our grunts became animalistic. He slapped my ass and it drove me insane. I bucked like a horse and screamed for him to fuck me in my ass. I wanted the intensity and passion to overrule the slightest hint of pain. When my body fell into an orgasmic state there was nothing I wouldn't do to keep that feeling.

We went at it like two dogs in heat. He pinched at my nipples, pulled on my hair, slapped his six inches across my face and I loved every minute of it. I think he did too because all the bitches, hoes, and hits I was getting made him cum all over me quite a few times. I think after his fifth shot over my body, he collapsed to the floor next to me.

"We need a shower," I whispered.

"Yes, we do," he replied in a miserable tone.

By the look on his face, he was trying to eliminate the worst mistake of his life. I didn't feel awful, but I didn't want him to feel he couldn't come back to me. "Would you like to join me or should I leave you here in your thoughts?"

"I think it would be best if—"

I cut him off. "Listen we can just act like it never happened. I'll take it to my grave only if you do one thing for me."

His worried face disappeared. "How much?"

I wanted to smash his head into the ground, but I knew this will all be blessing for me. I swallowed hard and said, "Nah, I got my own money. I just want to hold on to it that's why I don't live in the city. I thought about what you said about where I live and the respect thing. You were right."

"Okay, and now that your common sense side caught up with your smart side what do you want if it's not money?"

"I think it will be challenge for you. I need an apartment. Isn't it obvious?"

"Okay, where's the challenge?"

"I'm not paying more than what I am paying now and the rent can't go any higher after a certain amount of years. Oh, and if it does, it will only be decimal number percentage. How's that for a challenge? I'll let you mull it over." I went into the bathroom feeling confident that my situation had just leaped forward.

The warm water poured over my head; my mind was spilling of happier moments in the near future. There would be no more Quincy slapping me around beyond the bedroom. This would be the only way to keep him from show-ing up at my house whenever he felt like it. I would finally get some respect at the office by my zip code. I would probably be able to get car service now without question.

There was never any talk about that night until I saw him at my client's housewarming party. After Mark came through on our deal, my days at my firm became numbered. I sued them for discrimination and as I thought, they settled out of court. I made them sign a nondisclosure contract and received a letter of recommenda-tion. I left and within days landed an interview with Coplan & Daughters, the most respected law firm in the city, and was hired on the spot.

It had been almost two years until I saw Mark face to face again. It was better that way. If I needed his help I called him on the phone. There was a housewarming party by a client of mine; it brought our firm an easy five mil in billing alone. It was quite incidental that Mark sold him his first house. The house was so big that I didn't think I would bump into him; although, I would have loved to reenact every moment of our forgotten night. Only, if it weren't for the client introducing us for a hopeful business connection. My big mouth got me in a pickle when the client overheard my desire to purchase a summer house out in the Hamptons as well.

After the introduction to him and the woman on his arm our conversation was very much businesslike. I played my role as did he, but I was sure he didn't expect me to throw a monkey wrench into the game. I befriended his gem on his arm. I saw his eyes when I asked for an escort to the ladies' room. I took the opportunity to play the role of the woman with no friends and who hardly ever went out to rope her in. It worked because a week after we met she contacted me at the office to have lunch and since then our friendship had been building.

I secretly wanted her life and her position in Mark's life. I didn't know, nor did I care how long or serious they were. If befriending Regina put me closer to Mark, it was perfect. There was someone meaningful he had to meet, but I had to make sure it was serious and wouldn't fall apart.

10

Regina

How could that be? After calling to rush over here, then you just dismiss my presence. Is this meeting more important? What part do I play that's going to change everything? Has he finally changed his mind? There were many questions running through my mind as he showered. My phone sounded off, alerting me to an unopened message. I reached for a mug and poured some coffee for myself before retrieving my phone. Why was Mandie texting me at this time of the morning? I returned her text: What's up? Wit Mark. Can't talk.

I stood at the kitchen counter waiting for her reply then her messaged flashed on the screen: When is he leaving? We need to talk.

I knew what she wanted; she just wanted to be in my business. I was used to her pattern by now. Yeah k. Stop by before you head to court, I replied. Mark finally emerged from the bedroom dressed to kill.

"Damn, this must be big, huh?"

"Yes, it's going to change a lot and I am going to need your help. I plan on getting this contract signed this morning so I will call you with the details in about an hour or so."

"My help? With what?"

"If everything goes as planned I will have to sell out a building in thirty days. I will need you to make phone calls, send out e-mail blasts and, most importantly, get my corporate clients to see it."

"And when you do sell out what happens then?"

"I like your confidence in me. It means a lot. We'll have a big party when it's all said and done."

"Sounds good. I just hope the party isn't the only celebration in the works." I looked down to my ring finger, twirling the imaginary diamond around in circles.

"You never know," Mark said and kissed me on the cheek before walking out for his meeting.

I walked into the bedroom and tossed my purse into my closet then started to undress. As soon as I finished my shower and walked into my closet, I heard the service phone buzz. I threw my robe on and walked to the kitchen.

I hated that I had to walk to the kitchen to answer that fucking phone. "I told him to connect it to the land line so we can pick it up anywhere in the condo. He doesn't fucking listen!"

"Good morning, Ms. Peterson. Miss Amanda Sutton is on her way up."

"Thanks, can you let me know if Mark returns?"

"Sure will. Have a good day."

I placed the old school phone handset back onto its cradle and walked to unlock the front door.

I opened the door. "What is so important, Mandie?" I asked as soon as she stepped off the elevator.

"Mark isn't around right?" she answered me with a question as she stepped through the door.

"No," I said then stopped to look at her strange. She watched me up and down.

"Is this new?" She grabbed at the tied fabric strings.

"Girl, stop playing with me and tell me what the hell is so important that you just had talk to me about." I swatted her hand and gently pushed her toward the kitchen.

"Ooh, can you make some more coffee?"

"Yeah, sure," I said rolling my eyes.

"Okay, first don't be mad at me."

"That doesn't sound like a good start, Mandie," I said placing an empty mug in front of her.

"Mark called me."

My heart sank. "And?"

"I picked up the phone not realizing it was him. Now . . . "

I filled her mug with coffee.

"Thanks. I told him you were at a hotel—"

"You did what! Amanda, I thought I told you not to answer his call."

"I'm sorry, Gina, but he caught me off-guard. It was like six something when he called me. My first instinct was just answering the phone. I didn't look at the screen or anything."

"So what did you say?" If looks could kill she would have been dead.

"From your looks it seems that I fucked up royally. So when were you going to tell me you've been playing with toys on the sideline?"

Amanda was a good lawyer so I knew she could see right through me. *Damn!* I contemplated lying, but she dealt with liars every day. "Listen, Mandie, I didn't want to tell you anything because I didn't want you in my business, plain and simple. So now that you know what kind of lecture will you put forth?" I crossed my arms over my chest.

"Oh no, I have no lecture. Your business has always been your business. I just thought our friendship meant more than that. I thought you trusted me more than that."

"I do trust you. I just didn't want you to look at me funny." I didn't know what else to say.

"Well don't I feel like shit. My best friend of four years don't trust me enough to tell me she's fucking another dude besides her boyfriend. I guess next time I cover for you I'll return the same trust." Her words cut deep.

"Look, Mandie, we've been friends for a long time and I don't want this to change anything."

"How could it not? Answer me this, how many times have you used me as cover without my knowledge?"

My eyes fluttered, but I had to be truthful. "More than a few." I chuckled a little.

"Funny, huh? So are you going to tell me details? Was it just for sex or are you really planning on leaving Mark?" she prodded.

"There you go with your Nancy Grace shit. I'm not one of your clients. And just so you know it was only about the sex."

"Damn, I thought Mark worked you something awful. I guess I was wrong about his type. Maybe he's into some kinky shit and you need to bring it out of him. Ever tried roughing it up a little?"

Was she actually giving me advice? "No, and I know what he likes."

"I'm sure you do. Did he not say anything to you?"

"Yeah, he did and I told him the truth." My answer was a lie, short and to the point.

"Okay, I get it. You just got caught with your hand in the cookie jar and you feel you need to save face with me. I really don't give a shit what you do behind closed doors; I just thought we were friends. I guess I was wrong." She took a sip of coffee and headed toward the front door to leave.

I knew I should have stopped her, but weighing her friendship against my future was an easy decision. *Why didn't he say anything?* That was the only question on my mind and I wanted his answer sooner rather than later.

11

Vanessa

"I'm expecting someone else so I'll just have coffee for now, thank you," I said to the waitress. Norma's was one of my favorite breakfast hot spots. My frequency made me known to the wait staff; when I walk in I am guided to my favorite table, soon after my coffee will greet me and, depending on what day of the week it is, my order is already put in. It always felt good to be recognized and respected; it, also, didn't hurt that I had a shitload of money.

I opened my Hermès Cavalier tote and pulled out the manila folder with Mark's contract. I glanced at my watch; it was a little past eight. Lateness irritated me; there should be no reason for it if you left on time. *If he's not here in ten minutes this contract—*

"Good morning, Vanessa, sorry—" he interrupted my thought.

"Lateness can be prevented, please be on time." I hated to be a bitch, but starting off on an excuse seemed like a bad omen to me.

"Hmm, absolutely. Should we skip the pleasantries and get straight to the contract?"

He gave me the eye as he sat across me.

The waitress was right on his heels ready to take his order. "Good morning, sir, welcome to Norma's. Can I get you anything while you look over the menu?" She placed a laminated menu in front of him.

"Yes, please, a cup of coffee would be nice, thank you."

"You have a ten-day extension in here under your original percentage, that's not going to work. We'll be happy to grant the extension because of the time lapse of getting the building ready, but you have to lower your percentage. Another worrisome paragraph would be the bonus you so implied that you should receive if the contract was fulfilled."

"Ten-day extension under the same percentage you pay your Realtors. The bonus is strictly up to the seller, but it lets you know what I consider a bonus. In the same paragraph it also states the bonus is only implied if the contract is fulfilled in ten days less than the said time limit."

"I see, as the seller I decide whether you deserve a bonus or not. By the looks of it your bonus is only appreciated one way: cash. Honestly, I find that odd."

"I don't see that as odd. There's nothing illegal about it. What problem do you have with it?" He sipped at his coffee and looked over the menu.

I knew there was nothing illegal about it, but I wanted to read his reaction: very calm and bounced it quickly to me making me feel a sort of way for implying it. "No problem, just odd. Most bonuses are usually cars, trips, expensive items, you know something you would feel guilty buying yourself."

He laughed.

"What's so funny?"

"I guess I never looked at it that way. Maybe I should reword that part, what do you think?" He waved the waitress over.

I was getting a little annoyed by his old school business tricks. "Mark, let's just get this clear now because I don't want to bump heads later on. Stop with the tricks. I probably took the same business classes as you if not better. I too feel deceived or, worse, lied to. I like to lay it all out on the table."

The waitress arrived smiling looking to Mark. "Can I take your order?"

"Please, ladies first." He gestured pointing to me.

"Your usual, correct?"

I nodded my reply. "Mm-hmm, thanks."

"Usual, huh? What would that be?" He looked to me.

"Today is . . . Wednesday right? I think today is pancakes with one egg scrambled on the side and bacon."

"Okay, I'll have her usual too. Thanks."

I reached into my tote for a pen. Before I could sign on the dotted line his soft hand leaped to stop me. "Don't you want this signed?"

"Of course I do, but I would like to enjoy my breakfast first. Once that ink hits the paper I have to go to work. I would like to enjoy my meal because for the next few weeks I'm sure my meals will be thin to none. Don't you agree? Oh, damn there I go. I can't help myself. I have to throw it back." His eyebrows shifted.

I smiled at his honesty. I didn't know if he was flirting or just bullshitting to make me feel good. "So you're married right?"

"Umm, no and yes." He took a sip of his coffee. "We've been together long enough to be recognized by the state as married but, no, we have not undergone the big event where we profess our love to each while strangers, family, and

friends get drunk and have hookups in the bathroom or the bridal suite."

I almost spewed coffee all over the table from
my explosion of laughter. "Yes, yes, I've been to
some of those. Shit, I've seen it all. The bride
getting her last hurrah in the staircase near her
suite, the groom banging the bride's best friend
in the bathroom ten minutes before the bride
was set to walk down the aisle. Oh and I will
never forget the mother of the bride welcoming
her son-in-law into the family by blowing him in
the DJ booth, now that was classic."

"Damn, sounds like you've been to fun weddings. The most I saw at a wedding was the girlfriend trying to keep her presence on the hush
while she watched her man, the groom, have his
big day. It was funny because she kept moving
from seat to seat."

"Sounds like a stalker, honestly. So when will
you make it official?" I hoped for a small opening. I wanted to jump on him after smelling his
scent. Mark was dressed to impress; capable of
sweeping any woman off her feet by looks only.

"Umm . . . umm, I don't know. Let's get through
this contract then ask me that question." He
stumbled a bit so my door wasn't fully opened,
but it was unlocked and cracked.

"That's fair." The server appeared with our food and placed it in front of us.

"This looks great, thank you," Mark said.

We sat and ate over light conversation. After we finished I signed the contract and handed it over. "Well, it's official, we're hitched." I knew those words would affect him either in a good way or a bad one, but I loved to push people's buttons.

"I guess that means I will cover breakfast," he said with a smile.

There was still a hint of him flirting, but how far would he go? "I'm happy you know what's expected. Now, let's see if the honeymoon can live up to it."

"Okay, e-mail me the details and I'll have a messenger pick up the keys this afternoon before three with a copy of the contract for you."

I took my tablet out of my tote and swiped the screen. "I just sent it. You should get the alert shortly."

His phone whistled. "Yep, just got it so please forgive me, but I have to get going to earn that bonus. A VIP trip to Paris sounds good, but I like to fly chartered."

"VIP includes a hostess, are you willing to allow that?"

"Only if it's you." He dropped a few twenty-dollar bills onto the table then scooped up the contract and was headed out the door.

Yes, yes, yes. I have to have him at least just once.

12

Tony

"Hey, Diana, how's it going?"

"I'm good, Tony. I was just about to call you on confirming your friend on the next invite. You know we have to confirm. Since when do you bring clients to parties?"

Diana was the hostess at the masquerade party I took Regina to. Regina strong-armed me to put her on the guest list for a membership and since I was doing Diana secretly she wanted to know who exactly Regina was. Diana didn't know she was sex with one option: new business opportunity.

"Yeah, something like that. Listen when you send her the invite to the next event, I want you to blind CC someone. Will you do that for me?"

"What's in it for me?"

"Let's just say your next two nights will be filled so don't make any plans." *Got her,* I thought.

"Text me the e-mail address. I'll see you tonight at six. Don't be late because I don't want anyone else cutting into my time."

"Have you thought about what I asked you? I think we could make a lot of money and we could get some of my clients in front of the camera with a mask, that way their identities are secured. You can't tell me you wouldn't have fun."

"You know I can't purr without you, so you'll have to show me how. We can talk about it later."

"You know what happens when you talk like that. You might just see me for lunch." I grabbed my crotch calming myself.

"Send me the e-mail." The phone went dead.

There was something about Diana that drove me crazy; her sex was like no other. Her touch was always gentle and precise. Sometimes I thought she had the same career I did, but I was way off. She worked as a paralegal for a prestigious law firm in the city; her hosting parties only started a year ago. I've been a member since 2006 so I've seen many hostesses since.

Her flawless almond skin glowed naturally. Diana's piercing hazel eyes were captivating and would cause any man to empty his pockets willingly just to engage her even for a brief moment. Her body was toned, waxed to perfection, and she had her own hair; there wasn't anything extra she needed. Our first face-to-face encounter was a complete surprise and could have changed her life into something awful if I outed her.

It was two o'clock when tapping at my door awoke me. Who the fuck is this?

I opened the door and God had finally granted my wish. I rubbed my eyes to make sure it wasn't a dream. She was tall, standing in a short black trench coat with high stiletto boots on. Her garter straps were showing. Half her face was hidden by the mask covering her eyes; her bright matted red lips were tantalizing. My lips slowly moved into words: "Can I help you? Do I know you?"

She stepped forward unleashing her tied trench coat open.

"Umm ... umm ..." I was stuck.

"Let me show you." She gently guided me backward as she pushed the door behind her. My mini me extended to greet her happily.

This can't be real, *was the only thought I had at the time. I had no clue who she was, and none of my clients knew where I lived.*

She threw her trench to the floor showing her black lace lingerie exposing her perfectly sized breasts. "I've never done this before, but

I've been watching you. I'm the kind of woman who goes after what she wants and I just have to have you."

"Where do you know me from?"

"I'll tell you after. Now let me get what I came here for."

She kissed my lips, then moved to the nape of my neck. Her hot breath and warm, wet kisses brought chills to my body. She took both my hands and placed them on her breasts easing me back to the sofa.

"Have a seat," she whispered in my ear.

She climbed on top of me and inserted my manhood into her moist flesh. It felt like a perfect fit. Her movements were expert.

"Don't move, just enjoy the ride," she cooed into my ear.

I thought her tight, warm heaven couldn't get any better until she spun around revealing her impeccable round ass. I watched as she guided herself up and down my stiffness. I grabbed ahold of her ass cheeks and started to slam her down onto my pelvis. Her movements became faster and harder. Her moans became louder and more arousing to me.

"Yes, give it to me. Make me squirt all over you."

"Oh shit, you squirt?" My strokes halted for a second. I never had a woman who squirted and I didn't want to miss one drop. I flipped her onto the sofa to face me, spread her legs open, and dove into her like a jackhammer. I dug into her with no care and by her screams she enjoyed it.

"Play with it," she moaned.

I rubbed her clit as I stroked in and out of her flesh. By her groans I knew she was close to her climax.

"Yeah, I'm almost there. Rub it faster. Fuck me harder."

Three more strokes and she exploded all over. White, sticky cum shot straight out of her causing my mini me to drown willingly in it. I kept rubbing her clit and she just kept overflowing with juices. I finally hit my max and shot directly onto her breasts. Her body was shaking and so was I. I felt like I just came for the first time. Even I was shaking like a bitch.

It took me a few minutes to catch my breath, but I finally got the words out: "Now, who are you?"

I will never forget that night. She had been the only woman to make me shake. She made me promise to have an open mind before she revealed herself to me. She was the hostess of the exclusive parties I attended to acquire my clients. I didn't like that she just showed up at my apartment, but her actions gave her a pass. The next day I contacted the board of the building to enlighten them that their security was lax. The doorman was fired the following day. My home was my safety against anything. That was one detail I held to myself. Not even Regina knew where I lived and I loved her.

Diana provided that ultimate realm of satisfaction. It didn't hurt that she was very easy to please. After our first encounter worked out well for her, she didn't lose her job and I kept her on a weekly rotation free of charge. When the fifth week rolled in I wanted a little more and made her more useful than a weekly release of my toes curling up.

I pitched my wants as I bent her over. With every stroke I pumped into her my manipulation was effortless; having my cake with an option was definitely a plus in my book. As she granted me access to certain clients' private information for the past six months my client list became elite and provided a whole lot of money. With all the cash I had lying around I had to formulate a plan to open a business and Diana gave me the straightforwardness to do so.

***

I walked through the doors of Diana's workplace dressed in a sweat suit and a fitted hat. I pulled my cap down to shade my appearance along with a messenger's bag strapped to me. I pulled out a small padded envelope and walked to a familiar face.

"Hey, Stan, how are things?"

"You know, still got those bills." He eyed the envelope.

"I know how those are. Can you sign?" I offered an unfolded paper for him to scribble what floor the cameras were off.

THIRD FLOOR. RM 306, was scribbled on the paper. He used his eyes to signal to use the service staircase.

Meet me. Third fl. Rm 306. No panties.

I sent the text to Diana, rapidly climbing to the third floor. When I reached the third floor, I was ready for the high I got every time I was with Diana. I opened the service entrance to the third floor cautiously. I stood there to listen for a minute; then I heard the elevator chime open.

I stepped forward and watched Diana step out the elevator with her panties in hand. Immediately, I grabbed her and searched for room 306.

"Damn, what's the rush? We have an hour," she said.

"I know, and I want the full hour," I quickly replied locating the vacant room.

In my rush to open the door and get my fix on I didn't notice the completely naked ladies serving each other with their tongues on the makeshift bed of drop cloths splattered with paint.

"Oh my God. What . . ." Diana shouted.

I turned to the couple trying to divert my eyes from their scattering naked bodies.

"Ummm, this area is off-limits," one of the women said quickly trying to put her clothes back on.

"Listen we are all adults here. Yes, it's quite embarrassing to be caught in this situation. But we can all agree that our unexpected intrusion will never be spoken of. I just ask since we all are adults and I think you may like my suggestion so we can all be satisfied."

"Oh no, asshole, you're not about to watch me get off while you get off on all of us. No, thanks." She zipped her pants and with one swift movement pulled her shirt over her head. She stuffed her bra and panties into her bag. The other woman cowered in shame as she passed by Diana and me.

When the door closed Diana busted out in laugher. "Damn you, you don't care do you? You are out to satisfy yourself at all times, huh?"

"Come on, you would have squirted harder if you watched them too. Stop it. Now let's get to business." I wasted no time and pulled my erect penis out to get my fix.

13

Mark

It was three-thirty when the messenger finally showed up with the key to the building. I wanted to get the photographer there to take some test pictures for the virtual tour online along with my stage decorator to assess what we needed for a ready-to-show state. I made the necessary connections and headed out the office.

I hailed a cab and headed to SoHo to meet my team. I diverted Regina's calls most of the day with the excuse of trying to organize everything for the e-mail blasts. As much as I wanted to ask her to tell me the truth, I just couldn't bring myself to do it. I didn't want to leave her and I didn't want her to leave me. *If I marry her, will she maintain her secret lifestyle?* I sat back in the cab and replayed my lunch with Amanda.

"Why am I here Mark?" Amanda greeted me with hostility.

"I'm fine, thank you." Her readiness to assault me showed in her stare standing in front of me.

"I think you know me by now. I'm not one to sit and listen to the bullshit. Tell me why am I here. I think you provided me with a pretty clear picture."

She wasn't wrong, but I wasn't going to let go of her part. "Amanda, have a seat. I'm not here to oust you. I'm not here to hold it against you. I want to know the truth. I thought since she's been using you as a cover you can tell me what's going on." I played dumb for the moment.

She pulled out her chair and took a seat. Her eyes searched mine for some kind of tell of my motives. My poker face stayed in form.

"Amanda, my initial call to you this morning was to ask for your opinion on a ring for Regina." I knew that would tug on her violin strings.

Her entire demeanor changed before my eyes. She sighed then shuttered her eyes a bit, put her hand on her chest, and took a deep breath. "Mark, as someone who respects you and looks up to you I can honestly say she's not the woman you want to marry, at least not now. Give her a few more years. I think she needs to work out whatever she is going through."

"Can you tell me what she's going through?"

"I need a drink."

I waved the waitress over to take her order. I had to stay calm and not show any sign of devastation. I continued to appease her needs.

"I'll take a Bloody Mary, please," she blurted out to the waitress and dismissed her. "I'm sorry, Mark, I came here already agitated by an earlier compromising position I was placed in. I shouldn't take it out on you, but I also don't like that you have this cloud hanging over my head ready to drop golf ball–sized hail on me."

I did have my finger on the atomic bomb button, but if I opened my mouth to Regina my head would be served on a platter too. She was smart enough to know that much. "You know our secret will only bring us more problems than what we really want."

"Do you really know what you want?"

"Yes, I work harder every day to have everything I want. I'm sure you do too, now." I made it clear that I helped her in achieving some of her past accomplishments.

"You want the truth, then be ready to meet your true fiancée. You don't please her in the bedroom, she's been sleeping with who knows for how long, and only with you because she can walk all over you. I told you back then, she wasn't the one."

"And let me guess, you are?" It was typical of her to rub salt into my wound.

"Mark, I know we've always danced around what happened that night, but I know you liked it. Even after we all met you wanted it again. I see how jittery you are when I'm around, it's a sign of deception. And let's not talk about how many times you stole glances at my ass when Regina was around."

Now I was very uncomfortable and fighting to keep it bottled. "And if I was to tell you you're right, what then?"

"I would allow you to do everything you ever wanted to do with me." I slightly rubbed his leg below the table.

I had to laugh to release some of my uneasiness. "So I was right, you've been after me from the start. Who's to say you're not making all this up?"

"Mark, you can take it however you want, truth or slander. I don't think I have to convince you by her most recent actions. Now do I?" She gulped half her drink down.

"You better slow down; aren't you expecting a verdict?"

"Yes, but one of these won't do anything. By the time the verdict comes in, trust me, the slight buzz will be long gone. Thanks for caring, though."

"And I do care, but I don't think we can move forward with our friendship knowing your intentions. I love Regina and I'm sure, even after learning all of this, that she's the only one for me." I had to make sure she wouldn't get any bright ideas about coming between us for her benefit only.

"Okay, okay, I get it, you love her. Yada, yada, yada. I got the message. But do you think marrying her will change her? Mark, she's not worth the sacrifice. I'm sure she will never come clean or stop doing her dirt."

"Sacrifice? What sacrifice?"

"You know she can't give you all you want, that's all I'm saying." She grabbed my glass of water and took a sip.

"She'll be everything I need. Amanda, I understand that she's your friend, but just have the understanding we will never be. I don't want you." It was harsh, but her shit had to stop.

This eerie smile came across her face as if there was something I didn't know. "We'll see what you'll want."

"Sir, we're here." An Asian accent brought me back to reality.

I peeled off a twenty dollar bill and handed it to the cab driver.

"Need change?"

"No, thanks, keep the change," I said stepping out the cab. I saw the photographer at the door. "Hey, Steve, sorry for the last minute rush."

He extended his hand for a quick shake. "No problem, Mark, it's always a better payday when we work together. Peter just went to get some coffee at the deli over there." He pointed toward the green awning.

"Of course, well hopefully this will work out." I saw Peter approaching. "Come on, Peter, we have a lot of work to do with a very little window."

"I know, more like a pinhole in the dirt. Let's do it."

14

Vanessa

After signing the contract with Mark, Charles didn't let me breathe without an update and countdown via e-mail or text. As much as he said he didn't want me to cause any drama, Charles knew my type: caramel or cream, young and old. My phone alerted me to a new text message.

Did you get the date for Web blast? I want it up on our site once there's a confirmed date.

Oh my God, Charles, can I fucking breathe! It's after five. Since ten o'clock this morning he'd been on my ass for answers. He reminded me of our father more and more every day. I touched the screen of my phone and swiped to my phone log.

"Hey, Mark, I know it's still early, but do you have a definite date on the Web launch? There's a lot at stake here and my brother doesn't have full confidence in you."

"Hello, Vanessa, it's only been seven hours and everything is still in the beginning stages. You can't honestly expect answers this soon. You'll have to trust me."

"Oh, I'm not worried. But I do need something to tame my brother, sorry. I understand we are only a few hours into our contract, but I still have to answer to someone." My voice cracked a little. I quickly cleared my throat and apologized.

"This may not be enough, but we'll be staging the spaces and photography will be edited and proofed by the end of the day. I predict the launch will be favorable in two days."

"Two days?" I was in shock that he accomplished that much since my brother made the messenger wait until three o'clock even if he was there since noon. My brother was a dick like that at times. He thought the challenge was a game.

"You sound disappointed."

"No, I figured you would be on top of it. Although, you did surprise me with the launch prediction. I didn't know you still went to the building today. I didn't expect you there until tomorrow morning."

"Why wait until tomorrow if you can get a jumpstart today?" He chuckled lightly.

"Mark, did—"

His laugher went in and out. "Vanessa, do you mind holding for a minute? My other line is sounding."

"Sure, go ahead." I chewed on my cuticles while waiting for his return. He was intriguing to me. A lone Realtor quietly conquering New York's elite locations year after year and building his personal property ownership in vast amounts in a short time. I also found out that he was trying to close a deal in Ireland for one of his clients. It just so happened that his client was a friend.

"Sorry, Vanessa, what were you asking?"

"I was just wondering if . . . You know what, it's late and I'm sure you've had enough shop talk. So, I guess we'll talk in the morning. Thanks for the update."

"Umm, actually if you want you can come down to my office to see the test shots and a few swatches I need to approve."

"Where are you again?"

"Madison and Fifty-seventh, seventh floor. I'll be here for another hour at least."

"Sure, I'll be there in twenty." I ended the call and rushed into the bathroom to freshen up. I made a mad dash to my closet with the dress I pictured in my mind. It was black, not too tight to the body, and short enough for a second look. In my eyes every man gets excited when new temptation steps into their view. By his earlier flirtation I knew his office desk was about to be acquainted with my ass cheeks. I hurried out the apartment glancing at my phone's digital clock.

I despised lateness, but here I was arriving ten minutes past my expected arrival. There was a security guard in the lobby, but he didn't bother to inquire about my presence, just pushed the call button for the elevator. I anxiously waited. It took less than thirty seconds to get to the seventh floor. When the elevator doors opened, it was nothing I expected. It was modest, simple, and wasn't the only office occupying space on the floor. MARK SANDS was etched on to the double glass doors to a dimly lit entrance. There was no reception of any kind; it was furnished with a love seat and two armchairs facing each other. There was a small circular table off to the side with newspapers and a couple of magazines on display. I saw two other glass doors on opposite ends of the hall.

I walked toward the office where the light was bright. I knocked lightly and called out to him, "Mark?"

"Hey," he said and instantly looked to his watch. "I expected you here ten minutes ago. I know how you are about—"

"Okay you can go there, I deserve it. Just don't tell anyone or that bonus trip to Paris won't happen." I gave him a smirk stepping across the threshold. "So, show me what you have."

"I see you've already predicted my victory. That makes me feel good."

His eyes burned into me, igniting my desire. "Happy to hear I make you feel good." I stared at his lips wondering if they were as soft and moist as they looked.

"Why don't you have a seat here?" He pulled out the chair behind his desk.

I plopped my purse on one of the armchairs facing his desk. I walked around to his desk and took a seat in front of his computer screen. When he leaned down his scent made my flame light.

"Okay, so if you look here this will be . . . And this color will . . . Simple, lots of straight lines . . ."

His deep voice trailed off as I imagined him whispering in my ear and manhandling my breasts. He kept talking and I kept my eye on the prize: him. "It all looks good. Hey, Mark, is there anyone else here?"

I think he had an idea of what I had in store. Suddenly, he stood straight and moved back. I spun the chair around. "Is everything okay? Mark, let's be honest here . . ." I began to open my legs and it caused my dress to ease up a little. I reached for his thigh and squeezed it a bit. Damn, he was strong! By his manhood rising I knew he wouldn't deny it if I laid it on a platter.

As I was about to go in for the kill a woman's voice called out, "Mark, honey?"

Mark immediately rushed to the door to greet her with a kiss. "Regina, what a wonderful surprise. Great."

I couldn't see his face, but I was sure whoever she was saw my disappointment. "Hello. Well, Mark, I guess we'll continue this another time."

"Oh, Vanessa, please meet the love of my life, Regina. Regina, this is Vanessa Shore. She's my client on Greene Street."

"Hello, Regina, nice to meet you." I extended my hand with a fake smile as I rose from the chair.

"Yes, you too." Looking to Mark she continued, "I thought we could celebrate. I got us reservations at Setai in the financial district. Should I cancel? I mean I don't want you to stop because of me if you need to work."

"No, not all . . . Um, we were just wrapping it up. Vanessa, you're more than welcome to join us. After all if it weren't for you we wouldn't have anything to celebrate." He nervously laughed.

"Please, Mark, I'm sure we put the right man on the job. Besides"—I glanced at Regina then focused back to Mark—"I'll be by your side for the next thirty days, there's plenty of time to celebrate. I'm sure there will be plenty of late nights."

"Regina, what time is our reservation?" Mark asked quickly to diffuse the claws Regina was about to unleash by her facial expression. That was my cue to prance my no-good ass out of there; besides I didn't say anything that wasn't true. I just hoped that my forward actions wouldn't scare Mark's square, fine ass.

15

Diana

Our unexpected surprise threw me into a nervous wreck.

"Damn, I guess Stan has larger bills than I thought." Tony shrugged it off.

"Shit, I think I knew who that was," I said slightly covering the corner of my mouth.

"You better hope you don't." His little man wasn't at attention searching for his fix anymore. "Diana, we should get out of here. I don't feel like being questioned by security, which I'm sure she called just to spoil our fun since we ruined theirs."

I was ready to leave before any other unforeseen guests decided to intrude on us. "If it's who I think it is, then it could go either way. Let's go." I was completely rattled.

Tony grabbed my hand and led me out in a rush toward the service staircase. Nervously I looked around the empty staircase to make sure there was no one there.

"You okay? It's cool, the cameras are turned off on that floor so no one can replay anything. And I'm sure whoever that was doesn't want her secret out either." He wrapped his arms around me. I tried to shake the entire incident off, but I knew it was going to be hard.

I closed my eyes, and counted to three. "Yeah, I'm fine," I lied.

"I'll definitely see you tonight, right?" he asked with a sneaky grin.

"Yeah, just call me." I kissed him on the cheek unconsciously, not thinking of our strict agreement when in public even if we were hidden. I turned quickly and climbed up the steps to the fourth floor. I opened the door and walked directly to the elevator and franticly pushed the tenth-floor button. When I saw the fire-breathing dragon tattoo on her back it all came back to me.

I didn't think I would ever see her again. It had been close to a year since I'd even thought about that night. And of all places to see her again in that compromising position was not good. I didn't even know who she was, but if she was on that floor she had to work in the building. I put my Nancy Grace hat on.

The elevator doors opened at the tenth floor. I rushed past the reception area and headed straight to my office closing the door behind me. I walked around to my desk and took a seat, swiftly logging into the firm's directory. I looked through the board of directors, then the partners. If she was important to the firm her pic would be on the site somewhere. *How could I've not known that she works here?* As much as the firm loved to say they're fair and treated all employees with respect, it was the furthest from the truth. I didn't want my reputation tarnished just because I caught her with her pants down.

I kept hitting the down arrow, until her face filled my screen. My first instinct was to start looking for another firm. I was a paralegal so there were plenty of firms I could work for. I sat back and stared at the screen. *Did she forget who I was?* "This is not good, Ms. Sutton," I said out loud.

We met through a mobile sex app, but she wasn't open to any normal tryst. She was weird and way too aggressive for me. She wanted me to slap and damn near beat her before we got intimate. I wasn't into it and she flipped like a switch. Instead of her shy, seductive taunts she enticed me with, she went into a rage that scared the shit out of me. I didn't know if it was the alcohol or was she high making her act as if she owned me. When I told her it wasn't my cup of tea she threw a glass of wine at me and demanded that I suck on her nipples. As I insisted that she was not my type and turned toward the door she rushed me to the floor then hit me over the head with something. I only remembered the darkness that quickly came over me.

When I finally came to, I was completely naked, had a ten-inch rubber dick strapped to me, and was tied to her canopy bed spread-eagle. I couldn't scream because of the ball gag she placed in my mouth. All I wanted to do was get out. I was in a nightmare, a sick nightmare. I didn't know how far she was going to take it. I was terrified. In my mind at the time I envisioned men coming in and out having their way with me until I was weak. My fright made me still, so still that she removed the ball gag and untied me. My words were stuck in my throat. I didn't know what exactly she did to me, but by the stench in the room and the yellow wet spot I lay in I knew it definitely wasn't my kind of party. I remembered getting up, and wanting to reach for my phone to call the police, but when she handed me a white envelope stuffed with twenty Gs I stopped moving. I needed the money at the time in the worst way; my mother needed surgery and just lost her job. I'd moved back in with her to cut her bills in half. I'd just gotten my degree with only a potential interview for a job.

I took the money and left without another word. I felt nasty, worthless, but when I was able to pay for my mother's surgery I tucked away my regret and distaste for my actions. I was never put into a position like that, someone having full control and doing whatever kinky shit they wanted to me then shoving money in my face. That night I took five hot, steamy showers to get her piss-shit stink off of me after I took a whole lot of pictures and placed her underwear along with my clothes in a plastic bag. Insurance was important just in case it came back to bite me in the ass.

The choppy memories of the night were tucked away so deep, it never occurred to me what I would do if I saw her again. I never spoke or thought of that night until now. My life was good now; I had a well-paid job, my mother was cared for, I just bought a condo in the city, and my nightlife was more than interesting to say the least. I loved where I was at in life, but the greed wouldn't allow me to miss an opportunity to receive another payday for my silence. I was certain she didn't want her private interest on blast.

I clicked on her profile and wrote her number and e-mail address down on a Post-it then stuck it to the back of my phone. At the time my life was good, but thinking that a larger sum of hush money would make it better blinded me. I had all the evidence to prove it.

16

Regina

"So, that's Vanessa Shore, huh?"

"Yep, are you ready to go?" His eyebrows arched trying to read my expression.

"Sure." I kept silent and walked toward the elevator out of his office. I didn't want to argue because of my insecurity. I had to keep my cool, because he still hadn't told me what he wanted to talk about. I put my happy face on and pushed the call button for the elevator. I watched him lock up, looking for any clue to make me question him.

"I hope you didn't drive over here. Did you?" The elevator chimed at its arrival.

"No, I didn't. I know how you feel about driving in the city." I took his hand exiting the elevator. I wanted to ask him if *we* were okay. I was also waiting for him to ask me about last night.

As we stepped out the building a cab was letting out a passenger. He let my hand go to catch the cab. "Hey, hold on," he shouted to the driver.

I hustled over and hopped in with him. After he gave the driver our destination, he turned to me with a serious look on his face. I was already making the lies and excuses up in my head to throw at him.

"Regina, do you—" His phone sounded interrupting him.

If it's Vanessa, then there is no way she'll have a chance to be alone with him again, was my first thought. I tried to listen to his conversation, but all I got was "hmm-mm" and "yes." After fifteen minutes of his short replies he hung up the phone.

"Sorry, now where was I?"

"You were about to ask me something?"

"Ahh, yes." I hated when he played dumb. "Regina, where do you see us a year from now?"

I wasn't ready for that question. "Married." I answered with what I wanted now instead of my truth.

He smiled. "Well, every woman wants—"

"Here you are," the driver said.

"Thanks." He reached inside his blazer and pulled out his money clip to pay the cabbie. "Shall we?" He gestured toward the car door.

When we entered the restaurant, I gave my name to the hostess and she led us to our table. As we were seated a few minutes later the waitress came over to hand us our menus and took our drink orders.

I was nervous. I wanted it over with. I just couldn't understand why he wouldn't say anything to me about last night. Was he going to pretend like it didn't happen?

He took my hand in his. "You know I love you and at this point in my life I don't think marrying you will make me feel any different."

My jaw dropped. My eyes widened. *What does he mean? Is this supposed to be my proposal?* Where was the bended knee? I didn't see a box.

"If marrying you makes you happy then, why not?"

I didn't know if I should be happy or a little annoyed that he said it like he was buying me a house. Was it really that bad?

I tried to smile. "Why does it sound like I'm forcing you?"

"Honestly, you're the only one who needs that paper. I'm perfectly happy. Why aren't you? You still live your life the way you want." He waved the waitress over as if what he said meant nothing.

"Can I take your order?"

"Yes, we'll take the shrimp cocktail for starters, the porterhouse for two with a side of spinach and cauliflower mash for our main. Oh, and can we get another round of drinks as well? Thanks."

The waitress wrote everything down and took our menus away.

He took a huge gulp of his Jack Daniels and stared out past me. His facial expression changed suddenly. I wanted to turn around to see who or what made his eyes move side to side nervously.

"What is it?" I asked.

"Nothing," he said, but he kept staring past me.

Turning around would be so obvious and I didn't want him to feel that it was so important to me to know who he was staring at. "I'll be back. I have to go the restroom." I made sure not to look immediately. *I knew it!*

I calmly walked to the restroom cursing on the inside. *That fucking, bitch! I knew it! I wouldn't be surprised if she's sitting at our table when I return. Who the fuck does she think she is? Where did she get the audacity to assume he's a cheating, low-down, dirty dog?* I opened the faucet and washed my hands then freshened my makeup. "That shit ain't happening, bitch," I mumbled. I put a grand smile on and walked out the restroom back to our table. I made sure to slowly take my time getting to my seat just so I could put my eye on her.

Vanessa was sitting two tables behind us toward the corner with two handsome men. She was acting as if she wasn't looking my way. I smiled and waved hello. "There's Vanessa, Mark, did you want to go over there to say hello? Maybe we should invite them over here."

"No, I think I had enough of her for the day."

What the hell was that supposed to mean? Did he? He wouldn't, would he? I was so damn confused.

"Are you okay?"

"I'm fine. Why wouldn't I be? The man of my dreams conformed to my wishes. So where's the ring?" I squeezed my toes together to force my happiness.

"Umm, you want this. As you said I'm adhering to your need, but there are some stipulations."

"Stipulations? Is this a contract?" I took a sip of my Ketle One, not liking what I just heard.

"Yes, you want it, you pay, plan, and deal with all the necessary phone calls, tastings, scouting for venues all on your own. Just give me the date, time, and place to show up."

"I see, is that all? Are you sure you're okay with me making final decisions?"

"Remember, you want all that. I'm fine as I am now. You always need something extra." He gave me this strange look as if he knew something I didn't know.

Both our phones alerted us to new e-mails. He looked at his and swiped the screen. Mark's mood changed immediately. His lips were twisted to the side. His foot was tapping rapidly beneath the table. He started to guzzle his drink down. He stared behind me. *Was he really contemplating doing something with her? I should be pissed as hell right now. If I hadn't walked into that office when I had, her lips would be on his dick right now.* I kept breathing in deeply.

"I'll be right back. I should say something to Vanessa."

The waitress arrived with our main dishes as he stood up.

"Okay, don't let her keep you over there too long." I smiled to make him comfortable. It was so funny to me that she didn't want to eat with us when she was invited, but took it upon herself to be here anyway. *I don't like the way she's moving in on my man.* I waved over the waitress. "Can you send a bottle of whatever they're drinking on us?" I motioned to the table Mark was now sitting at.

"Sure can. Can I get you another?" She picked up my empty glass.

"Sure, but can you make it Patrón on ice instead? Thanks." She smiled and took the empty glass away.

I watched Mark laughing with Vanessa and the notion of jealousy snuck in. My mother always told me treat your enemies kinder than you would treat yourself. I smiled as the waitress brought the bottle over to the table, which should have been Mark's clue to get his ass back to our table. It still took him ten minutes to waltz his way back. I finally checked my phone to stop the e-mail reminder alert. You're invited to our next event was in the subject line.

As I opened the e-mail Mark returned. "Thanks for sending the bottle," he said taking his seat.

I deleted the e-mail and put my phone down. "No problem."

"Anything important?" He looked to my phone.

"Just junk. Now can we get back to discussing our wedding?"

He twisted his lips. "I thought we discussed it already. You want it, you plan, pay, and make all necessary decisions. There is no further discussion."

"Okay, what about my ring? Isn't that on you?" I forced a smile.

"That will be the one thing I will handle."

"Should I call the jeweler with my expectations?"

"No, I think you have enough to keep busy."

"So, we're really doing this, huh?"

"I'm simply complying with your demands, but you know what this means right?"

I didn't like his tone nor his words. As much as I beat it into his head that marriage was our next step, I was sure I didn't want the step after. Acting as if he was a brokering a deal instead of inputting his thoughts and ideas on an event that would change our lives forever was discouraging. I pushed my plate forward, annoyed by his blatant disregard about my feelings.

"What's wrong? Aren't you hungry?"

I wanted to leave, but leaving would only cause the bird in the corner to peck away at him. "I'm not." The waitress returned with my drink and I emptied the glass within a blink.

"I thought you would actually be happy about this. Why aren't you? I thought this is what you wanted."

"I am happy, but my happiness is short-lived by the way you're acting. Is this just another deal or is it something you would like to share in? Because if it's all up to me and my final word on everything, oh and let's not forget my money, then why are we doing it if your interest is little to none?"

He laughed.

"I don't find anything funny, Mark."

"Absolutely nothing is funny, Regina, but lately it's been so hard to make you happy. You have unlimited access to money, mine or yours. You have an option to work or not work. I don't hound you like I should when you spend the night at Amanda's house." He quoted the air. "I give you what you want and you still find something to be unhappy about. Maybe we should just—"

Does he know more than what Amanda told me? I will kill that bitch! "Should what? Leave each other?" My heart was pumping faster.

His nose crinkled and he completely stopped eating his meal. "Really, is that what you thought I was going to say? First, that was the furthest thing from my mind. I'm shocked you would say that. Second, I was about to suggest we elope. There would be nothing to plan. Why were you so quick to suggest we leave each other?"

He has to know something if he's talking reckless like that, I thought. I knew what would turn everything around. I thought of my mother, which always brought tears to my eyes in a hurry. "I can't believe you." I stood up in dramatic fashion and stormed out of the restaurant. I quickly hailed a cab and hopped in.

It was wrong to do, but something was wrong. I gave the driver Amanda's address. This was serious. I didn't want to lose Mark. He was the love of my life. Yes, I'd cheated, but we were not married. If we were married then I'd get rid of my double life. Do away with it for good. He just couldn't leave me. The tears became real. I knew then, Mark was the only man for me for the rest of my life with nothing extra. I closed my eyes and prayed that God would forgive me for all the wrongs I've done to this man. "I promise, I vow to be the perfect wife. Just help him get past this episode of my weakness," I whispered.

17

Amanda

"Good evening, Ms. Sutton, Ms. Regina Clay is on her way up."

"Thanks, Simon." Regina was the last person I expected. What the hell was she doing at my door?

I heard the knock at the door, walked over, and opened it. "Hello, Regina." By her expression, she wasn't here to mend a friendship.

"What the hell did you tell Mark?" She had fire in her eyes.

"Do you want something to drink?" I turned my back and walked toward the kitchen to put some water on those flames she was shooting at me while I figured out a plan. Telling her the truth might ruin everything. She was the only female I didn't feel the need to control and the game I played with Mark challenged me; getting him just one more time would do the trick and then I would have him forever if he wanted it or not.

I finally heard the door shut and her footsteps behind me. "Amanda, I asked you a question. I didn't come here to drink," she demanded.

"First, don't think you can walk into my house and be loose at the mouth. That shit will get your ass slapped real fast." My strong Brooklyn roots surfaced.

Her eyes widened and her shoulders relaxed. "I'm asking you again." Her voice was much calmer. "What did you say to Mark?"

"I told Mark exactly what he needs to hear." I looked to her left ring finger. "Wait hold on, did he not ask you to marry him?"

She was surprised. "How did you know that?"

"Because after I told his ass off about you staying at a hotel he finally got it through his thick skull that it was the right thing to do," I lied.

"Did you talk to him after my conversation with you this morning?"

"How could I? I was at court all day." I pulled out a bottle from the wine rack. "Now, do you want a drink?"

She started to laugh and cry all at once. "I . . . I . . . I . . . thought you told him everything. I thought I was going to lose him."

I opened the cabinet and retrieved two glasses to pour the wine into. "I wouldn't tell him. I'm taking it to the grave, that's what friends do for each other."

"Yeah, you're right. I owe you an apology, I'm sorry. I didn't want to be judged. Everyone thinks I have such a perfect life and how Mark is Mr. Wonderful, but a woman's needs are a strong, impulsive, erratic ball of electricity fighting to be released."

She lifted her glass as I poured the wine. "I get it. There are certain things you must do to keep what you have."

"Sure I'm crazy for doing it, but it makes us better. It makes me better."

I nodded my head and gulped my full glass of wine down. If she thought I actually cared then I should have received a nomination from the Academy. I continued my act with the "you're not wrong" and "you have every right" spiel to get her comfortable. She sang like a sweet little bird, spilling all her sexual endeavors. I continued to fill her glass as she went on about everything. She told me about Mark wanting her to pay for the entire wedding because she wanted it not him. I told her she shouldn't sacrifice the only event in her life that's meaningful. Why shouldn't she have the wedding of her dreams?

I would want it, regardless of how I had to get it. I convinced her since she couldn't give him the one thing Mark really wanted she should go all out for the only thing she wanted.

"Hey, Regina, how come you don't adopt? I bet if you agree to that he'll change his mind about the wedding."

"Mandie, I don't want to have a baby. I'm not ruining my body. Do you see some of these women out here after kids? Their stomachs are never back to normal and if they are that means they live in the gym. I don't do muggy, sweaty balls and ass recirculated air."

"If your ass was fat and losing your breath after a flight of stairs you wouldn't say that, trust me." I didn't know that she was so shallow. She went on and on about how kids are so much trouble and take away so much time from your life. Regina was selfish and didn't know how to hide her true feelings after a few drinks. I heard her mumbling, but it wasn't clear. Her voice kept going in and out. I looked to her on the sofa and she was fast asleep.

My first thought was to call Mark, but I thought it would be better if I sent him a picture instead. Actual proof was better. I didn't want him to think I was lying to him. He already thought I was. I stood up and removed the empty bottles of wine from the coffee table to the kitchen. I walked to my bedroom and heard my phone ringing. I looked at the screen and it was an unknown number.

"Hello?"

"Hello, Ms. Sutton, I hope I wasn't disturbing you." The female voice was soothing to my ears.

"Who's speaking?" I asked very curious for the answer.

"It's not necessary to know now, but let me jog your memory. It cost you twenty Gs to keep me quiet. I personally think letting you acquire what you have was more beneficial to me. I'm ready now to negotiate a more permanent deal."

My mind went numb. Who the fuck was this? What the hell was she talking about? "First I don't negotiate deals with unknown callers." I pushed End on the screen. Did she not know who I was? Then to play silly games with me over the phone after midnight, I was pissed. *If I find out that one of those motherfuckers from the office did this as some kind of hazing shit, I'm going to kill them!* My message alert chimed from my phone. I looked down and swiped the screen. Message Downloading. I waited for the picture to download.

Pink lace stained underwear appeared on the screen with the caption, Aren't you missing this?

I stared at the picture then another appeared to be downloading. What kind of sick initiation shit was this? A round, plump, bruised ass showed on the screen. *Ouch!*

Unknown Caller popped up. "Listen, if this is some kind of prank, it's going to be real awful for whoever put you up to this. I know those assholes don't have the balls to do it themselves. I hope you didn't do this for free." I waited for who I thought was some young intern to fess up.

"No prank. This is very real. What would happen to your partnership if your little sick secret gets out?"

I hurried to my bedroom door to peek out at Regina on the sofa; she was still sleeping. I started to pace the bedroom floor racking my brain for clues. Who the hell was this?

"I'm that one 'i' you forgot to dot. Meet me at the closest Dunkin' Donuts spot before court on Monday." The phone went dead. *Monday? Today is Friday; that gives me more than enough time to find out whose life I have to destroy.*

This bitch didn't know who the hell I was or who I had at my fingertips. It only took one phone call to my investigator to send me everything on my prankster. I had her entire life in my inbox in less than an hour. When I scrolled through the various attachments I stopped at her DMV photo. I stared and stared nothing came to mind. I clicked on the Facebook link in the e-mail. When I saw her profile picture, then it was clear as day.

Shit! Shit! Shit! How could I be so forgetful? This will sure cause my ass problems if this isn't taken care of quickly and quietly.

18

Tony

It had been two weeks since I'd seen Regina. She was on her shit again, not picking up my calls, ignoring all my direct messages, rejecting my e-mails. What the fuck was her problem? *Oh, let me guess, her man must finally be acting like he gives two shits!* I had to get to her. I woke up early one morning and went for a jog. I found myself across the street from Regina's condo watching everyone who exited and entered. After an hour I saw Regina. Her hair was different, short and blond. I started to approach her. The hood of my light windbreaker was over my head covering my face a little. I got closer as she walked away from the front of the building.

I didn't want to scare her. I whispered her name so she would turn around. "Regina." She stopped abruptly, but didn't turn around. I whispered her name again. I saw her shoulders move up and down slowly taking in big breaths.

"What are you doing, Tony?" She still didn't turn to see my face.

I walked to the front of her to look into her eyes. "Regina, can you stop playing the games?" She nudged me to the side, but I held my ground.

"Keep walking, Tony. I'm done. I'll be married in six months. There is no more us or future. Your services aren't necessary anymore. Didn't you get the message when I didn't show up to any of those parties or return any one of your unheard voicemails?"

"Regina, when are you going to be honest with yourself? You've told me before that you were in love with me. What happened? Mark will never make you happy. He doesn't understand your needs. I do." I stepped closer putting my face less than two inches from hers. I smelled her minty breath hoping she would give me a sign. Just when I was about to taste her lips she turned her face and stepped back.

"Tony, what don't you understand? I don't want this to continue. Stop calling me. Don't seek me out. Move on. There's no promises or hopes with me. What don't you get?" She folded her hands across her chest.

I saw the seriousness in her eyes. I was hurt. The need to have her in my life surpassed her rejection. I gently touched her face and kissed her forehead. "I'll let him have you for a little while, but I promise you that you'll never marry him." She didn't push me away so I knew there was still a chance.

"Tony, you were paid for what we had, a lot I might add. Now, you need to move on to your next sugar momma because I'm no longer sweet. I can make things very difficult for you. I don't think you want that, do you?"

Her brows shifted showing her disdain in me at the moment. There was something I had to do. "Did you know that Mark attended those parties?" Her eyes darted side to side, confused.

"Stop it okay? Your lies aren't going to work. He doesn't even know about that life. He wouldn't even associate with anything like that. I'm not stupid, Tony."

"Okay, you would like to think so, but he has been there enjoying the pleasures you once sought after. I think he would love to go with you, don't you? You guys can discover amazing things together. Maybe I will let him know how much you would enjoy it." Hopefully my threat would make her realize the mistake that lay ahead.

"Are you threatening me? Do you actually think he would believe you? You're nobody. Your degrees fell short after high school. Do you think your lies will work?"

"My education has nothing to do with anything and I resent you for saying that. As you know my pockets are deep enough for you and many others."

"Of course, I paid you enough over the past year. Or maybe that's it: you're losing your biggest hitter. Is that it, Tony, you're upset about losing your potential earnings? How much will it cost me for you to leave me alone?"

I laughed. Regina was never aware of how much I was worth. I was sure she would be surprised to know my unclaimed father was one of the biggest builders in New York.

"Really? I love how you make everything about money. Trust me I have enough money to make you happy. Make me understand how is it that one month you're ready to fuck me anywhere, anytime then the next you're ready to stick me back into the closet. I think you like that game. Like I've told you before, I need you in my life. I can't just turn it off. If the problem is my career, then I'll let it all go, for you."

She laughed in my face. "If that's what you want to call it. Tony, we are done. Period. The end. There is no more. Show up again at my home and I'll file a restraining order against you."

"And how will you explain that to your future husband?" She wasn't serious. She didn't want her secret out.

"This is not a threat or request. Now please lose my number and forget you ever met me."

She walked off staining me with hurt and an open wound. My heart was sinking. How could she do this to me? I loved her. Regina had to know Mark wasn't who she really wanted. I needed to get Regina out of my head and I knew the perfect person: Diana. She was the only person who could distract me from Regina. If I allowed it, Diana would have my heart.

19

Diana

My palms were sweaty, turning the corner to Dunkin' Donuts. *Maybe I should just turn around. Maybe I should just forget about this.* My thoughts were distracting my purpose. I had to pull it together. I shook it off before entering the coffee shop. I went directly to the counter and placed my order. I tried not to look around searching for someone. I was sure she was there already although I was thirty minutes early.

I casually walked to the pickup counter and faced the morning crowd, probing their faces for Amanda. I glanced to the guy behind the counter rushing around putting sandwiches in bags and making lattes. When I turned back to the sitting patrons my eyes locked on Amanda sitting by herself in the far corner. She had on all black, shades on, and her hair was pulled back into a tight, smooth bun. I grabbed my latte and headed over to her table.

"Good morning, Amanda."

She immediately removed her sunglasses. "Wow, you cut your hair. It looks good, Diana."

My knees almost buckled and the latte nearly made it onto her lap. How the hell did she know my name? I was sure she never knew my name. When I used those sex apps I always used a fake name. I clenched the chair tight, hoping I heard her wrong.

"Surprised? Don't be, it's obvious to me now that you have no clue as to who I was. Please take a seat." Her voice was calm with no hint of anger or hostility.

I didn't think this through. I'm fucked! I felt my eyes darting back and forth to the door waiting for my feet to comply with my brain. Amanda put her briefcase on the table and popped it open. Did she have a fucking file on me? Damn, she was good.

"Maybe . . ." I started to backpedal on my earlier intimidations. "Amanda, I don't—"

"Oh, but you did, Ms. Wells, so now put on your big girl panties and follow through. Would you like me to go first?" She pulled out a manila folder and smiled as if this was a case she was prepping for.

I felt my sweat building in my armpits and above my lips. I sipped at my hot latte shocked at how thick the folder was. *Damn, does she have my entire life in there? It could very well be a ploy to scare me. Stick to your guns. Stay in your game. You are in control. It's her career in jeopardy,* I repeated in my head, before opening my mouth. "Ms. Sutton, I hope that file isn't all about me. It looks like you went through a lot to get that. Two slices of cucumber does wonders for dark circles around your eyes." I smirked eager for my insult to piss her off.

"Thanks for the suggestion. Now let me offer one to you." She flipped through the pages in the folder and stopped at my mug shot when I was seventeen years old. "You really changed your life around since then, but you still have a wild side don't you?" She turned the page to another picture.

"Where did you get this?" I grabbed the picture to closely examine it. She wasn't supposed to have this. How the hell did she get this?

"I don't think it matters where I got it. Do you know our firm's HR policy? I'm sure you don't, most just sign it. If a partner or the head of your department suspects drug use, you will be subjected to urinate in a cup and sent home until your results are in. Most higher-ups don't care about this because the many who do are fully functional like yourself."

I was steaming and ready to throw my coffee in her face. Instead, I uncovered the lid of my latte and poured it over the paperwork she had in front of me. "Fuck your pictures and all this you got from sealed cases." I stood up and walked away.

Fuck her! Where did she get that picture from? When I posed for the second picture she showed me, my state of mind was damaged. I thought it was the only thing I could do to make extra cash. It was just pictures. I was assured that the pictures would not be produced or developed in any shape or form. I was embarrassed, ashamed that someone else saw me in that position. It's not a good look if your extortionist was caught with her pants down in the worst way.

I decided on calling out sick for the day and headed back home. Oh shit, what was I going to do now? When I got home I cried my eyes out over the humiliation and disgrace I just endured. That one picture of me crumbled every hard bone in my body. How was I going to turn this around on her? She was at the top already and I wasn't nearing her inner circle any time soon.

Two days passed since my encounter with Amanda and I still had not gone into work. I was scared she would magically appear on my floor ready to divulge any- and everything about my past. I knew all my cases were sealed but the question was, how did she get her hands on them? What judge did she know? Cases that old you had to physically sign for with a judge's consent because it was not computerized. I had to find out who signed for them.

I sat in my bed with my laptop open staring at a blank screen. My front door buzzed. *Oh, damn I forgot!* I reluctantly got out of bed and headed to the intercom pad close to the front door. "Who is it?"

"Can you let me in?"

It was Tony. He could be a blessing in disguise. "Yeah, okay." I buzzed him in and cracked the front door. I rushed back to my bedroom, grabbed the tissue box, and emptied it onto the floor. I heard the front door close and footsteps walking toward my room.

"Hey, Diana, are you sick?" He sounded concerned.

I blew my nose with one of the tissues on my bed and threw it to the floor. "Are you going to take care of me?"

"Only if you want me to."

I smiled.

"I tried calling you, but you didn't answer." He took a seat on my bed. "We never finished our conversation about my proposal to you. I'm ready to go. I have another place to set up all the necessary camera feeds. I figured using your house was out of the question. It's easy money, but without you it won't last. Have you put any thought to it?"

I totally forgot about his little plan to exploit my position as hostess to the elite. It was a good idea, but my ass was on the line if anyone figured out I was stealing their private info to entice them into a new outlet for their desires. I looked to him with tears in my eyes. His brows rose confused. "Tony, I may not be able to help you as much as I would like. I did something stupid, real stupid."

"What did you do? Come here." He wrapped his strong arms around me. "Tell me, what did you do?"

"I was greedy, Tony. I thought if I had more money to put into this, you would see how serious I was. I didn't want to be just the person to help you. I wanted to be a partner and take in just as much money as you."

"Forget that, just tell me what you did so I can help you fix it."

I closed my eyes, knowing that he wouldn't be able to set his plans into motion without my help. My unlimited access to exclusive clients was immense compared to his depleting client list. I found out from the other hostesses, who he tried poaching, that they were too scared and loyal to conduct anything with him, business or pleasure.

I saw my future with Tony, although sex was the only quality he saw in me. If the sex only happened once he would not be a thought in my mind. After months of passion it becomes emotional whether you want it or not. There were times where it was just that: sex. Then there were more times where sex wasn't the priority. We laughed about the wild and crazy shit his clients made him do, we talked about anything; there was something there, I felt it.

Spilling everything about my meeting with Amanda and what I wanted out of it soothed me. I didn't hold my past back from him. I told him about my mother and all the things I did to keep her with me. I hoped my sorry tale of half-truths and misleading information would make him feel for me.

"It's okay, Diana. I think I have the perfect plan."

20

Mark

I wasn't going to chase after her. *She's probably going to that sex party, anyway,* was running through my mind. I put on a huge smile watching Vanessa and eating my steak. I was happy that Regina interrupted Vanessa's obvious come on. I was sure if I'd walked over there and asked her to meet me out back she would have jumped at the chance to add drama to my life. I was a huge flirt and that's as far as I would go. I learned my lesson and would like to keep that to myself.

After I finished eating I paid the check and headed home. I expected Regina to be there. I wanted her to be there. I needed her to be there. I turned the lock. "Regina, I'm sorry." I was a wimp; she had my heart no matter what she did. I deserved it; she had every right to step out since I did. I learned to deal with Amanda being around; I just made it clear I didn't like her very much. My reasoning was rational in my mind; what she didn't know wouldn't hurt her.

No one answered. I walked through the entire condo. She was nowhere to be found. I reached into my pocket for my phone and swiped the screen to Regina's number. I pushed Call. It went straight to voicemail. Maybe I was right, maybe she did go to that fucking sex party. I didn't bother to leave a message. I removed my suit and tie and got into shorts then headed to the bar hidden in the living space. Pouring a full glass of twenty-year-old Scotch I thought would settle the anger brewing within.

A couple of hours passed and half the bottle of Scotch went with it. I checked my phone: no alerts. I wasn't mad anymore. I was more regretful and ashamed of what I did with Amanda. It was long ago and I was happy that she kept it to herself. I really had to commend her and should have been more tolerant of her friendship with Regina. It was two in the morning and no calls or messages from Regina. As I picked up the phone an alert pinged. It was a text message with an attachment.

She's not doing anything. She's drunk and passed out! Come get her in the a.m.

I smiled. Regina was sprawled out on the sofa, arm hanging off the edge. She didn't go! It meant a lot to me that she didn't go. I didn't like it that she was over there, but it was better than where I thought she was. I slowly stood up; my head was spinning with the room. I quickly sat down to slow the room down. "I guess I drank more than I should've."

I woke up the next morning with a stiff neck and a slight headache. I tried to stretch out my neck to relieve the tension, but it only made it worse. "Great!" To my surprise I heard the door unlock.

"Mark, did you leave already?" Regina called out before the door slammed shut.

"Whoa, can we keep it down a notch? I know your head is hurting just like mine. Please."

I saw her look to the Scotch bottle. "One of those nights, huh?" She dropped her purse and took a seat next to me.

We sat in silence for a few minutes.

"I'm sorry, Regina. I don't want you to feel spending the rest of my life with you is a chore. I also don't want to feel as if I'm not enough. Am I enough for you?" I looked directly into her eyes. "I love you unconditionally no matter what you do."

"Of course you're enough. Why are you asking me that? I'm pissed that you don't want to be involved in any way."

Her eyes darted back and forth from me to the framed picture of us on the wall. I had to understand why she did the things she did to me. I reached for my phone and swiped the screen to my e-mail. I opened the invite. I must have opened this a million times last night staring in wonder. It was very secretive. There was only a number and some simple instructions. When I called the number a very explicit message was heard: "Fuck Me If You Can event will be held tonight. Please confirm attendance no later than nine p.m. at 669-6780." I placed it in her lap.

Regina picked up the phone and started to cry immediately. "Please, Mark, please . . ."

"Please explain this. It's important that you tell me the truth." Her face was red and the bags under her eyes were more noticeable.

"It's . . . it's . . . it's . . ." She was caught and her expression gave it away.

"Don't lie to me, Regina, tell me what this is."

"It's an invite to a party. An exclusive party." She started to walk away trying to leave it at that.

"Party? It's more than just party. I know what kind of party this is. Now tell me why are you're getting invited to these types of parties? Tell me, Regina, have you been with someone else?"

"How do you know what type of party it is? And how did you get this e-mail? Did you go to one of these parties? Are *you* seeing someone else?"

Typical of her to turn everything around on me. "There you go. It sounds to me like someone's darkness came into the light. I fucking called the number."

"Mark, you don't know what you're talking about. It was a party I was invited to and when I went I saw what kind of party it was and left. Now, they e-mail me all their events. It's not an issue. Question is how did they get your e-mail address? You must've gone to one yourself for them to send you an invite. So which is it?" The tears clearly stopped, and her glare was piercing.

I knew what she was doing. "Regina, you're not going to turn everything around on me. I don't know what you're doing behind my back. We've already started our life together. We've already lived as husband and wife for years, and only because this marriage certificate is so important to you, I'm willing to go through it. But we can't move forward if you can't tell me the truth."

"I'm not doing anything behind your back, Mark. I want to be married, but not like this. I feel like I'm forcing your hand. I mean, telling me I would have to decide and pay for everything sounds obviously forced. I don't want that."

She was right. I didn't believe any of Amanda's accusations and if I was going to do this then my heart needed to be in it 100 percent. "I do want it, but I want everything a marriage has. I want kids. I don't want to adopt. I want *our* kids and there is a way it can be done. Are you willing to give me everything?"

Regina's eyes closed. "You know I can't have kids. Why would you—"

"We can have kids. There is a doctor in California who can make it happen. We may have to relocate for six months, but that doesn't matter. We can afford to do that. I may have to make some trips and forth, but I don't care about that."

Her eyes opened with defeat. "You really want kids? Do you know how hard it will be? How can you be sure this doctor doesn't take your money for six months and blame me for not being able to have a baby? I'm not willing to be put on an emotional rollercoaster. Are you ready for that outcome?"

"Yes, are you willing to take that ride with me? I can't and won't do it without you." I was on pins and needles waiting for her response. If she said yes, then my life would be complete. If she said no, then I would learn to live with a missing puzzle piece. Her silence worried me. I grabbed her hand and looked into her eyes. "Can we just try?" I couldn't read her expression.

"As long as this wedding is a combined effort not just one-sided. Agreed?"

I pulled her into my arms and hugged tighter than ever. "You've just made me the happiest man in the world. My hangover has disappeared. How's yours?"

She pulled back and tilted her head. "How did you know I was drunk?"

"Amanda."

"Of course. What did she say?"

"Nothing. She sent me a picture of you passed out on the sofa. Why don't you go take a shower while I go get us something to eat, then we can go pick out your ring." I landed a big kiss on her lips and headed to the bedroom to throw on some sweats.

I spent the rest of the day with my future wife. My credit cards were being worked to the max even after the $1.5 million I spent on her engagement ring and wedding band. I, on the other hand, opted for the simplest band: no diamonds, twenty-four-karat white gold with our initials inscribed on the inside. We stopped at all her favorite showrooms and she placed orders for the next two seasons.

While she raved over the next season's designs I called the doctor in California and set an appointment for the next week. I noticed the excitement was not there. *How can she not be excited? We're about to have a family.* I had to shake the negativity in mind and concentrate on the positive. I was going to have everything—a family.

21

Vanessa

Making Mark eat his words was the last thing on my mind. Making sure he sold the property out was my priority besides getting a taste of him. His first clients should have called him already to put a bid in. I only hoped he didn't take it personally since he met them the night before. Yes, there was a possibility of damaging our relationship businesswise, but I didn't care about that. I would've had him if his girlfriend didn't walk in on us. Well, maybe that was a good thing or else there wouldn't be a relationship at all from her near-murderous glares she gave me last night.

Maybe I came on too strong, but I loved seeing her squirm, defending her territory as such. The game of getting the prize was the ultimate desire for me to conquer. The hint of her knowing my intentions enticed me even more. I wasn't ashamed of what I did or what I was known for. My brothers were though. Charlie always seemed to pick up the pieces after I demolished the secret sanctity of life's moral compass. Honestly, it was more fun when they were married. The rush of getting caught, lying, and scheming just to get it on was in fact the high I craved.

I tried dating regular guys; it never seemed to work out. There was always an emotional tie: needing more access to my life, emotions, displeasures, future goals, etc. When they already had an emotional attachment to someone else the hunt was on. There wasn't any satisfaction if they weren't attached. This way there was no need to divulge my life's goings and comings, future goals and achievements. If it weren't for my family my butt would probably be living abroad hiding from all the hurt I'd caused. Everyone had a price and it never surprised me when the wife or longtime girlfriend took the lump sum to keep their mouths shut and wait until I was ready to give him back.

I didn't wake up every morning and say, "Let's see whose life I can fuck up today." The only men I felt on common ground with were those who were already seasoned in their prime. Some were easier to tamper with than others and then there were those who took discretion to another level. I didn't know why these games gave me such a thrill, but I surely wasn't about to stop. My wealth was enough to spread around; besides, my tenacity wouldn't allow me to stop. It was part of my persona for the moment. Settling down wasn't on my calendar anytime soon.

I was sitting in my office thinking of Mark when my fingers involuntarily dialed his number. It rang three times before it was sent to voicemail purposely. "Hello, Mark, I wanted to check in with you and see how everything was going. I hope I didn't cause any trouble with your wife. It looked as if she left abruptly. Anyway, call me when you can."

That was strange. He had a thirty-day deadline and the clock was ticking; why wouldn't he pick up the phone? I had to be honest with myself; his wife made me curious for the first time. By her eye cutting and fake interest, I didn't have any doubt that she was well aware of my objectives. When she didn't make an uproar upon her entrance, it had me questioning myself: What was her game? How was it that they'd been together so long, yet he hadn't married her? She wasn't ugly or out of shape so why hadn't he taken her off the market yet? There was something holding him to her. What was her flaw?

I wanted to find out her last name so I could look into her, but I would have to go to my brother, Charles. I wasn't going to ask Mark; it would only make him reconsider my main purpose. It wouldn't be my fault if his girlfriend/wife found out; that would make him sloppy. Since my intent was clear to her, she should be working out a defensive plan. It was only fair I knew who I was playing against. *This should be fun!*

22

Regina

Two days had passed since Mark purchased my ring. It was eight carats, round shape, color grade D, and internally flawless with an ideal cut. I walked away after I told Mark that was the one. I didn't want to hear how much it cost. I knew the right questions to ask to ensure the rings that were put before me came with hefty price tags. The band was simple, diamonds all around, same clarity and equaling four carats. It was something spectacular to see. The brightest rock I'd ever seen. It was grand. It was perfect.

Even with the atmosphere shifting to my enjoyment there was still the precarious position I walked in on. Did she not know he didn't have a weak bone in his body? She would definitely have to step up her game. I expected to be treated with respect. The Mark I knew wouldn't fall for a trap like that. I prayed he knew better. There was still a 10 percent doubt after he showed me that invite.

There was only one way to get that: a member had to vouch for you. *Who did he go with? Was he there?* After that whole incident I unsubscribed to the e-mail blast and never saw another invite. I had to keep my promise to God. I was going to be the perfect wife. No more.

Mark was out the door by six this morning to meet clients for back-to-back meetings starting at seven o'clock. It was just a little past seven when I finished my coffee. *His meeting shouldn't take longer than an hour each*. Today I was picking up my ring. *A surprise brunch with his future bride would be perfect to show it off*, I thought. I stared at my empty ring finger and said, "You won't be bare anymore."

Its radiance reminded me of how much money was put forth for my happiness. "It's perfect, Giovanni, just perfect." I wallowed in the envy brewing around me. I held my hand out displaying its beauty.

"Is Mr. Sands around?"

"No, is there a problem? He told me I could pick it up today."

"No, no, there's no problem. It's paid for in full the day you picked it out. I would just feel a bit more comfortable if you had an escort. You have rare beauty and—"

"Say no more, Giovanni, I understand fully. Do you have a car service you trust?" I smiled at his concern.

"No, but if it's okay with you I can have my nephew take you home or have it delivered to Mr. Sands this afternoon."

"Giovanni, you're so kind. It's not like I'm taking public transportation or anything, but if you insist, you can have him walk me to the garage across the street."

"It would make me feel better. I wouldn't want anything to happen to you because you stepped out of my store with a new accessory."

"Giovanni, it is insured, correct?"

"Of course, but Mr. Sands would never forgive and I would lose his business altogether."

"I get it. Go ahead and get your nephew."

"Thank you, Ms. Clay. Can I offer you anything while you wait? It'll be about five minutes before he can escort you."

"No, I'm fine. Just don't keep me waiting. I want to meet Mark before he gets all tied up."

"No problem. Have a seat."

I couldn't stop exhibiting my new addition. I already felt the hate piercing my skin.

"Oh, that's beautiful, honey. That's nothing but love or a 'I fucked your best friend, please forgive me' ring," an older woman said approaching me.

No, she didn't just say that! "It's only love, nothing as low as that. It was my pick."

"Congratulations, but take it from me, you will be paying for it one way or the other. Take it from someone who's experienced it all. He'll throw it in your face one day. If he doesn't then you, my dear, have found a man every woman has dreamed of."

Before I could discredit her blatant jealousy, Giovanni appeared with the younger version of him. "Ms. Clay, this is my nephew Anthony. He will escort you to Mr. Sands."

I extended my hand to greet his nephew. Then I turned to the woman talking smack. "Will you need an escort after your purchase as well? I will be more than happy to wait for you." I smirked at her.

She smiled and said, "Oh no, darling, my escort owns the store. Hello, Gio."

Well, she shut me up instantly. I took what happiness I had left and walked to the door with Anthony following close behind me.

"Knock, knock," I said as I tapped on Mark's office door. I pushed the door open to find him sitting at his desk distracted by his computer screen. He didn't even bother to look up. "Hello, Mark." I held my hand out showing my ring off.

"Hey, what are you doing here? Were we supposed to meet?"

He was very surprised, but didn't even notice the ring. I held my hand directly in his sight. "Hello, Mark," I repeated.

"It looks great. Do you like it?"

"Nope, I love it. Did you have something to eat yet? I thought maybe we could grab some brunch or something to celebrate and we could set a date."

"Honestly, Regina, my time is so thin right now. I—"

There was another knock at the door. "Mark, I thought—"

Of course, I should have expected it! By the look on Vanessa's face, her immediate plan was spoiled. "Well, hello, Vanessa, it's good to see you again. Did you guys have a meeting planned?" I made sure to causally smooth my brow with my ring finger.

"Oh . . . um . . . I was in the neighborhood and I just thought to stop by to check on the latest buy offer."

She was lying straight through her teeth. The bag she carried told me different, but if she wanted to play we could. "Oh my goodness, what do you have in that bag? It smells exquisite."

"It's just some platters my chef put together for me."

"The latest offer? Vanessa, I talked to Charles this morning both meetings. I'm sorry I should have called you right after."

"Well, Mark, why don't we go into the conference room, eat some of that food, and you guys can discuss the offer. Vanessa, I hope I'm not imposing on you. I'm just starving right now and at this point robbing anyone for a bite of something is not beneath me." I laughed, covering my mouth with my left hand.

"Wow, Regina, that's a beautiful ring. You weren't wearing that extraordinary piece when we met. Is there a congrats in order for you guys?"

"Thank you, yes, we finally made it official. So, Mark will be completely removed from the market and adulteress eyes." I giggled, hoping my subliminal words were loud and clear.

"I know what you mean. Congratulations to both of you. Mark, do you have time to go through the offer with me now?"

Mark's expression was priceless, watching two females staking their claims without a screaming or pulling hair throw down. I didn't think he'd ever been in a situation like that before. His body language showed me that he was too scared to move let alone agree to anything Vanessa said in my presence. It was best I took the lead. "Mark,

I'll show her to the conference room, that way you can wrap up what you were working on." I leaned over his desk and kissed his lips. "Don't take too long or else Connie will have to order you something from downstairs."

I grabbed the bag out of her hand and guided her to the conference room.

"Wow, I didn't expect this," she blurted out.

I turned off the nice-nice attitude. "What's that supposed to mean?"

"Nothing really, just an observation." Her tone changed as well.

"Let's see what you were trying to seduce my future husband with," I said emptying the bag. "Wow, caviar, eggs Benedict, smoked salmon, a bottle of champagne, hmmm, you went all out huh? It's still warm." If looks could kill she would have been dead five minutes ago.

"Excuse me? Seduce your future husband?"

"Vanessa, you're not fooling anybody especially me. So stop trying to put Mark in a compromising position."

"Don't tell me you're not sure of which side he'll end up on? Warning seems a bit insecure."

I was ready to back smack her and throw her food behind her. I restrained myself. "Oh no, you just don't know Mark. He wouldn't, at least"—I cut my eyes at her—"not with you." She had to know I wasn't stupid. I was positive I ruined another attempt.

"I wonder what prompted such an extravagant dedication since a few days ago it was bare. Maybe it's a cover for what's in store." She took a seat across from me and dropped her $15,000 Hermès tote on the table. I only knew how much it cost because I had one myself.

"So are we going to continue to play nice or will I have to show you what's mine is certainly not up for grabs? If you're looking for . . . let's say some affection I can give you a number. He's into a whole lot of tricks just like you. He's costly, but don't worry he's worth it so I've heard." I gave a chuckle.

Vanessa's brow rose as she put her hand over her mouth. "I'm surprised you would be on someone's rotation instead being the first."

Was she dumb? I had to wrap this up before Mark walked into a cat fight with words. My cool wouldn't be the only thing lost. "Listen I get you want to fuck my man, but since I've called you out on your game then bow out as a real woman because next time you won't just receive a bottle."

"Okay, so what do we have here? Ahh, man, this looks great, Vanessa. Thanks, I hope my wife here didn't impose. Please, if this was meant for someone let me know. I can have Connie get something delivered over there. Too bad it won't be as good."

"No trouble at all. My chef spoils me. Please enjoy."

"So what brings you on this side of town? Aren't your corporate offices downtown? I could've sworn Mark mentioned that to me." I saw Mark's eyes widen.

"Yes, but I had some business to attend to near here. It was convenient. Is there a date set?"

"Yes, my birthday. I want it to be special and I don't want to get clocked over the head for forgetting it either," Mark replied with speed.

I kept a poker face. *We never discussed a date. There could be only one reason why he's so quick to pull the trigger. He knows that I know where her boundaries lie.* I stuffed my mouth to keep me from reacting to his response.

"How sweet and smart. Regina, don't take it personal, most men forget meaningful dates."

I stopped chewing to throw her an annoyed smirk then continued eating ignoring her words.

"So, Mark, do you have the paperwork on that offer?"

"Yes, it's right here for you to look at." He handed her a manila folder. She didn't open it; instead she looked at me in a calculated way.

"I'm really sorry to do this, but I have to. Regina, please don't take this personally, but can I ask you to leave? My legal department would kill me if they found out you were in the room while we were discussing pending offers. You do understand don't you?"

I almost bit my tongue. I had to put a smile on and suck it up. "No, I completely understand, an agreement was signed. Sure, can you refrain from business for just a few more minutes, though? I'm almost finished eating."

"Vanessa, I think she's okay."

Was he begging her? "Mark, it's fine. We can talk about the wedding for a few minutes. I'm thinking Greece or maybe somewhere in the Caribbean, what do you think?" I asked rubbing it in.

"Wherever you are it's okay for me."

"Awww, that's so sweet, you two must be so in love, but you have to tell me what took you so long to ask her?" She was so manipulative.

"I wasn't ready." I halted her third-degree assault toward Mark.

"I guess every woman is different. To each her own," she admitted.

I refrained from shooting off at the mouth and simmered my temper with my last bite. "Mark, please don't make it a late night. We have a lot of things to do before heading to California to pick our prospective surrogate." I shouldn't have given her any ammo, but deterring her persistence was on my mind.

"Surrogate? So you guys are having a baby as well?" Her fake smile burned me.

I pushed my container to the side and took Mark's hand in mine. "Yes, we are having a baby. Two if we're lucky." I forced my joy squeezing his hand.

"You can't have kids, Regina? That must've been a struggle for you as a couple, in the beginning of course."

Okay, she was reaching too far into the cookie jar. This had to stop or I was going to literally slap her head off. "Okay, I think you've been subjected to enough of us. I'll let you two get to your business. It was nice seeing you again, Vanessa. Maybe you'll be able to attend our wedding?"

"Oh I'm sure it will be beautiful, but unfortunately weddings are like hot, flowing lava for me."

I had a sneaky suspicion why. I held my thought in. "Well, honey, I'll see you later." I gave him a long kiss good-bye. *That should slow her tempo down.*

I walked out of the conference room straight to his secretary. "Connie, first, you know I don't normally ask you anything, but, if you could, call me when she shows up or has any meeting with him? I don't trust that bitch. Mark I'm sure of, but her ass is definitely dangerous around my future husband."

With certainty my cage was rattled, but she wasn't going to intimidate me into falling back to watch her destroy my impending future.

23

Tony

If Diana did everything I told her to, Amanda would no longer be a problem for her. As I told her before, humiliation will always knock them off their high horse. It was almost eight, and the night held a lot of slick talking to put Amanda where she had to be. The bait was me so it all seemed simple enough. I pulled my phone out and dialed Diana to see where she was.

"Hey, are we on schedule?"

"Yup, she just left. She should be at the restaurant in twenty minutes," she whispered. "Are you sure she's going to fall for this? She very well could see this coming."

"Did you do everything I asked? If you didn't, tell me now." I was irritated by her doubt.

"Of course I did, but why did you want me to look at this place in SoHo?"

"Just be sweet, sexy, and very interested. Okay? Make sure to put on a good show," I reminded her.

"But I still don't understand. Who is this guy to you?"

"That will be clear as long as you do your part."

"Don't worry about that, I can handle myself. I just hope you can." She was concerned about Amanda denying my gift to verbally woo women of their feet.

"Did he confirm the showing? You did make sure it was during the day? And you made it clear that he had to show you the place not an assistant or some inexperienced broker only looking for commission?"

"Yes, yes, and yes. I got this. You're not worried are you?"

"Just as much as you are about me. I'll talk to you soon." I hung up feeling confident. I took a last look at myself. "Custom-made suit, hair perfect, Rolex, money clip, and lastly business cards." I opened a square container on my dresser and ran my fingers over the divider labels. "Export buyer and seller, maybe. Sports agent . . . Oil dispenser, perfect." *This should pique her interest*. I grabbed my keys and phone then headed out the door.

***

The Uber car service pulled up in front of the restaurant. "Thanks, hopefully you'll be in the area when I'm ready." I stepped out just as she arrived; it couldn't have been timed any better. I hurried my step to open the door for her. "Let me get that for you," I said smiling. Her hair was wrapped into a low bun, exposing her diamond-studded earrings. The red formfitting dress hugged her every curve just right. Her ass was solid; there was no sloppy gelatin bouncing as she walked.

"Thank you," she replied not paying me much attention.

I gestured for the hostess to seat her first, and play her role. It all determined her tip in this cameo.

"Mr. Tatum, how are you? Are you sure? Your table is ready, and the wine you've requested has been set to breathe." She didn't bother to address Amanda at all. It was as if she wasn't even there.

Another hostess arrived nudging Amanda a bit just to shake my hand. "Mr. Tatum, so happy when you're in town. I'll let the chef know you're here."

Amanda stared me up and down before saying, "Wow, you must be a whole hell of importance, because she hasn't even looked at me."

"I'm sorry, did you have a reservation?" one of the hostesses asked.

"Yes, it should be under Simmons. I'm supposed to meet a client here."

I stayed silent, waiting for my cue.

The hostess swiped at the screen in front of her. "Are you sure it was reserved under that name? I don't have any reservations by that name."

"Can you try Ms. Sutton? I had a temporary assistant all week and she's been screwing up royally." She was quick to throw blame to cover her embarrassment.

The other hostess turned to me. "I'm sorry, Mr. Tatum, would you like to be seated now?"

"I'm sorry, it's not here. I can offer you a table next Thursday at eight. How does that sound?" the hostess asked.

"Ms. Sutton?" I eased my way to her rescue. "I would like to offer you my table."

"I can't . . . I mean . . . I'm supposed to be meeting a client here." She was blindsided by my chivalry.

"It's fine, but are you sure your client will be here? If the reservation wasn't made I'm sure your client was not informed as well."

She agreed. "I just don't want—"

"Please, I insist. It would be my pleasure to have you as my honored guest."

"I don't have dinners with just anybody." She was defending her obvious plotting as she eyed the hostess.

"Maybe you would feel better if you knew my full name, Daniel Tatum." I reached into my blazer and handed her my business card.

"Oil Dispenser?" Her eyebrows raised. She quickly searched her tote and pulled out her phone. "Anybody can get business cards made." She placed her phone on speakerphone and dialed my number in front of me.

I was prepared. I knew what I was doing; too bad she didn't know what would hit her in a few hours. I didn't make any movement. I calmly smiled and allowed her to play into the game. My voice was heard: "You've reached Daniel Tatum, please leave a message and I will get back to you shortly. Thank you."

"Now, let's take our seats."

"Only dinner." She smiled as the hostess led us to our booth nestled into the back corner, isolated from the other diners.

"Do you drink red wine?"

"Sometimes, depending on the year."

"How does 1958 Giuseppe Mascarello Barolo sound?" I didn't think she knew anything about wine.

"Italian, fruity, hmm, that's a pretty good pick." Her pearly whites showed again.

She seemed impressed. One point on the board.

"So what do you do?"

"I'm a defense lawyer," she answered.

"I thought so. You have a very strong presence. Maybe that's why I had to have dinner with you. By the way, thanks for not shooting me down, that would have been pretty embarrassing."

The waitress arrived with the bottle of wine and poured a bit into my glass for tasting. I gestured her to continue and serve Amanda first.

After the waitress filled our glasses she quickly disappeared and Amanda's confused look made me have second thoughts.

"Okay, so why haven't we seen menus yet? What kind of restaurant is this?" She tasted her wine.

"I don't eat from the menu. The chef will come to the table to let us know what he'll prepare for us. Ms. Sutton, can you leave the lawyer persona at the door? Please let's just enjoy each other's company." I tilted my glass toward hers.

"Ms. Sutton?" She raised her brows as if I shouldn't have said her name.

"Yes, Ms. Sutton, you never fully introduced yourself to me."

Her cheeks flushed red. "Oh my God, you must think I'm so rude. My name is Amanda

Sutton." She took another sip from her glass. I looked to the waitress to keep her glass full.

"No, not at all. You're as rude as any New Yorker. I'm used to it."

"Are you here on business or coming back from business?" She changed the subject quickly.

"I live in Dubai, Los Angeles, and New York throughout the year. Most of my business is done in Dubai."

She snuck a quick peak at my ring finger. I laid my left hand on the table for her to examine with her glances.

"Wow that must be hard on your family."

"Actually, no. It's just me."

"I don't believe you." She playfully giggled. "There's no way you're single and straight!"

I laughed. "Should I be offended? I know a well-dressed man may seem suspect, but my stylist dresses me. I can't take credit for it, although sometimes I wish I could."

"So do you distribute oil to refineries for purchase? Or do you go around like a salesman presenting your product to accumulate buyers?" She seemed interested.

"All of the above. I own a few oil rigs around the world so I'm always selling and buying. But enough about work. Can I ask what you do for fun?"

"Hmm, let's see . . ."

"If you must think about it, I'm guessing you haven't done anything fun lately."

"You're absolutely right." She sipped at her glass as I barely touched mine.

As long as she keeps drinking, it will be easier than taking candy from a baby, I thought smiling. "You're beautiful and definitely need to have fun before you forget how."

"I could only imagine what you do for fun," she said seductively.

Is she already putty in my hands? She can't be this easy, I thought. I could see the chef approaching followed by a server holding a tray.

"Mr. Tatum, how are you? And you, madam? I'm Chef Myrie," he greeted us extending his hand.

"Hello, Chef, nice to meet you," she said returning his light handshake.

"So, Chef Myrie, what's on the menu?" I jumped in.

He allowed the server to place the small plates in front of us. "These are just a few appetizers I prepared. They include all your favorites, some shrimp, some veggies, and a little bit of seared Kobe beef. Your main course will be my new favorite, curry lobster with small slices of Wagyu beef on a bed of greens. Excuse me, I haven't asked your guest if she's allergic to anything. Usually, you dine alone." He looked to Amanda.

Amanda was too busy focusing on the food wafting through the air to even notice his concern.

"Amanda, you're not allergic to anything are you?"

"Huh? Umm, no not at all. This smells fantastic."

"Great enjoy. Your main courses will be ready in thirty minutes."

"Thank you, Chef Myrie, I know you'll bring us your best." He left the table giving me a thumbs-up behind Amanda's back.

Chef Myrie and I went way back since high school days. He came from old money. The day he graduated, his father bought him this restaurant. Even when he was in his teens he traveled abroad learning how to perfect his craft. We'd always been close so when I started my career of pleasing the ladies he afforded me just the place to wine and dine my clients. Depending on who I entertained, his services were always a great touch.

"This is great, Daniel. I gather you dine here all the time with your significant other."

"I love his dishes. Chef Myrie worked with the finest in Europe, Japan, and Spain, but his specialty is a classic with a twist. He has all his signature dishes on the menu if you're not comfortable with what he's serving." I avoided her implication.

"Not at all, I'm fine. So, you have a place in the city?"

"No, I prefer the suburbs. I do stay in the city, but it's never more than a night. I'd rather that my neighbors be at least a mile away. Besides, New York has the craziest city life Sunday through Sunday. That's not me. I like my privacy."

After a little question-and-answer conversation, and another bottle of wine along with dinner, she was ready for picking.

"Amanda." I stroked the back of her hand gently.

"Daniel," she cooed.

"Can I show you how I like to have fun?"

"Now, Daniel, I'm not that easy. You can't expect me to fold after a couple bottles of wine. Now can you?" she said slapping my hand.

"Have I been a bad boy?" I encouraged. After what Diana told me pain was my definite in.

"You like to be punished?"

I felt her feet easing up my leg. She took my hand in hers and guided it to her mouth. She licked and sucked every finger as her feet rubbed on my stiff manhood. Amanda was good, but I was better. I removed her feet and scooted closer to her.

"Can you tame me, Amanda? Can you handle me?" I whispered into her ear and pushed her hand toward my crotch.

"I like to punish naughty boys, can you handle that?" she grabbed at my hardness.

I pushed my hand between her legs and pressed on her clit making her feel some pressure. Amanda's nipples poked through her tight dress forming perfectly round bumps. Her girls were ready to play. I pressed harder at her seed almost forcing her to moan. I felt her moistness when I teased her entrance. I pushed and pulled at her lace underwear until I ripped a hole exposing her wetness. I kept teasing her as I nibbled on her ear.

"I want to punish you and make you taste every inch of me," she moaned loudly.

I squeezed at her clit causing her to shake and spread open her legs wider. She was dripping like an open faucet. Her expressions and loudness were transparent; I could have had her right there if I chose to. I decided on heading over to the hotel room to continue my pleasure phase with her.

"I think we should leave before we get kicked out. Let's get out of here." I removed my hand from her warm, wet spot and licked it clean.

"I think that's a good idea." She quickly scooted out the booth waiting for me anxiously to meet her needs.

As we hurried out the restaurant, she couldn't keep her hands off of me. When we got into the cab, she unbuckled my belt and yanked my dick out. She devoured my stiffness without a word from me. She sucked and jerked on until I exploded in her mouth. After she swallowed every drop she kissed me, pushing her tongue forcefully into my mouth. It was disgusting, but I tolerated it since there was a bigger motive. When the cab pulled up in front of the hotel she was the first one out the car. On the ride in the elevator her sadomasochistic ways started to erupt.

She slapped me across the face. "You better bend me over and shove your cock deep inside me."

If Amanda thought she was going to smack me around and squeeze on my balls for the rest of the night, I had another surprise for her. We were both going to feel the pain.

24

Diana

After talking to Tony and seeing the smut film he secretly created I was more than willing to do him any favor requested of me. If making some Realtor blush made his life easier then so be it. I made sure to set the appointment for during the day with the Realtor. Whatever Tony had with this guy, it was his business and none of mine. The only plot I was thinking of was Amanda's humiliation and the amount of money to sell it off for.

Amanda may have thought I didn't know any-one, but I had my own resources. Tony wasn't the only one helping me behind the scenes. There was a young twenty-year-old college dropout, Fenton, living next door to me who helped me out from time to time. He was the one who found Tony's address for me, so I could put my moves on him. It turned out Fenton was a genius hacker; he sold his talents for hire and buried his life in between codes and a select group of others like him. He was very isolated and socially awkward. I felt sorry for him and befriended him. He never had visitors and always had delivery service for everything. I believed I was the only one to enter his apartment. I thought his place would be smelly with empty boxes everywhere but to my surprise it was immaculately kept. I never saw him take garbage out or even get the mail. His skills provided me clues to Amanda's so-called untainted life.

It was just before noon as I waited for the Realtor to show me this place. A cab pulled up and a handsome, tall man hopped out.

"Hello, sorry for the wait."

"Oh no, you're right on time. I'm Diana." I extended my hand to greet him.

"I'm Mark Sands, it's my pleasure. Shall I show you the space?" He opened the entrance to the building.

I made sure to show off my assets as I walked ahead of him to the elevator. "So tell, Mark, how many potential occupants do you have for this space?"

"Actually, this is the only space available. All other spaces have been contracted and have already moved into escrow. Are you looking for a client or yourself?" He pressed the PH button on the elevator as we entered.

"A client. He's very private and wants larger space. I'm surprised you haven't gotten a bite on this. I was sure when I made the appointment you were going to call me back because you found a buyer."

The elevator chimed and the doors opened to the top floor. There were two apartments on the floor. We walked to the door labeled PH-A.

He took me through the penthouse showing me all the exquisite marbling, top-of-the-line appliances, floor-to-ceiling windows exposing all the views of the city's skyline. The place was staged with furniture so it wasn't hard to bait him into taking a seat next to me on the bed as he showed off the spectacular views.

When I looked out the window I spotted someone standing in a vacant apartment directly across. Then it hit me: Tony just wanted him in a compromising position. I lay back on the bed. "This feels good. C'mon, Mark, lay back and enjoy this small moment with me. I'm sure you don't get many breaks in your day."

With much hesitation he lay back. We were looking up at the newly painted white ceiling when I made my move. I turned to the side facing him. "Mark, tell me, have you ever christened any of your places before?"

"What do you mean?"

I thought he was playing dumb. I pulled my front zipper down my dress to my belly button, showing my intentions. I guided my hand along his muscular arm and past his belt buckle. Before he could refuse I climbed on top of him. "C'mon, those marble counters in the kitchen would put you at perfect height." I rocked back and forth slowly, then lowered my lips to his.

He grabbed my wrists and pushed me back forcing me to sit up.

"Don't fight it." I kept moving my hands and inching forward to his lips.

"Stop it, please," he yelled.

I kept rocking and fighting him to give in to me. I could see the flashes bouncing off the mirrored closet facing the window. I didn't think Mark even noticed until he pushed me off him with force.

"What the hell!" He quickly moved to the window. "What the hell is going on here?"

"I—"

"Who the hell is taking pictures? Who the hell are you?"

I got up from the floor and zipped my dress back up.

"I'm calling the police." He reached into his blazer and pulled out his phone.

"Please don't. It wouldn't be a good idea. I'm leaving now." I rushed out without looking back almost knocking a woman entering the apartment. I did what was needed.

It was my first day back at work since my meeting with Amanda and I was looking forward to it. I had a backup, thanks to Fenton, if my first attempt to collect didn't work. I typed on the keyboard and opened a new e-mail. I retrieved the flash drive I tucked away in my purse and plugged it in. The video Tony made was chopped into two-minute playbacks. I attached the first two minutes to the e-mail and sent it to Amanda anonymously. Fenton created a dummy e-mail account for me so she didn't know it was me. I also had him hack her account to copy her contacts on to the drive as well. I wanted her to think I was scared and wouldn't try to extort her with all the dirt she had on me.

I waited five minutes; then it became ten minutes. No response. I sent her another two minutes with a message: Fifty thousand or the entire sixty minutes gets sent to all your contacts.

It was less than twenty seconds when the response came in.

Who is this? Where did you get this?

Another response came in within seconds: Who is this? I decided on making her sweat this time. I waited ten minutes before sending my reply.

Sixty thousand.

I figured jacking up the price would light some fire under her to ask the obvious, where and when, but it felt more like I was giving her too much time to have second thoughts. I scrolled through her e-mail contacts, selected her assistant's address and sent the first two minutes of the video. I CCed her on the e-mail expecting her to take me seriously. It worked because within seconds of sending the e-mail she responded, Where and when? Cash in hand.

I smiled. *Yes, gotcha, bitch! Just wait for what else I have in store*. I made her wait for my reply. Revealing myself now would be stupid so instead I typed, Washington Square Park by the fountain @ 10 p.m. I figured the meeting place was perfect to get an edge on her. The night crawlers there always looked sketchy.

Suddenly, I received a text from Fenton. There was an attachment. When I opened it my jaw dropped; it was a picture of a young toddler. *Fenton came through all the way. One of these days I have to shake him off a little something-something just for being so good to me. This is going to be a bigger payday than I thought. Now I have proof, not just a birth certificate. This should make her ass squirm a little more.*

25

Amanda

How could I be so stupid? How could I not see this coming? It was too easy to have my way with him! I hated myself, now it was going to cost me sixty Gs to eliminate this threat. It was minutes after two and I still had one more client to meet with. The money was not the problem, but getting it would be. My safe at home held twenty-five tops and getting to the bank would be impossible to withdraw the funds before closing. *Shit!* My fingers tapped on the screen of my phone. *Fuck!*

My assistant walked into my office and closed the door. I knew what was coming, but when I saw the video it was easy to mislead what she saw.

"Ms. Sutton, I . . . I . . . I don't know how to say this—"

I laughed to make it seem as if it was just a big joke. "Jeanine, I already know. Someone sent you a video of me in, well, let's just say . . . not a position you've seen me in before, nor would you want to." I paused watching her body language. She sat up straight, her hands intertwined, twiddling her thumbs, right leg bouncing, eyes welling up with water. "First, it was not me in that video, she was an actress made up to look exactly like me. It was all staged."

She covered her mouth and she bowed her head.

"It was brought to my attention that someone on staff has been exposing my strategies and client information. As you know all employees have signed a nondisclosure once hired. It's rumored you were sharing such information for money. Now because that video was sent to you ten minutes ago and you walked into my office to inform me, it tells me that you're not the one. With the cat out the bag, there has to be some secrecy with my investigation meaning if you discuss this with anyone within this firm or socially you can kiss your job and future good-bye."

She started to cry. "Ms. Sutton, I . . . I . . ."

I grabbed some tissues and walked around my desk to hand them to her. I took the seat next to her and saw how shaken she was. I had to deceive her at every angle. She was young, not very confident in herself, was hired on a temporary salary for a full year and finally hired as a full-time employee as of a month ago. Now I had her scared shitless for her job and questioned her relationships personally. I needed her to be nervous if she wasn't already. "Listen, Jeanine, you've worked for me for close to a year. Soon I will be partner and in order for me to bring you with me I must know that I can trust you unequivocally. I can, correct?"

"Oh, Ms. Sutton, you can trust me," she said through sobs. "I just opened the e-mail. I didn't even watch the entire video. As soon as I saw your face, I mean your impersonator, I . . . I closed it immediately and deleted the e-mail permanently from the server."

I had her too terrified to say or do anything. "Jeanine, don't worry about anything. I see a bright future here for you. Why don't you take the rest of the day off, go to the spa on me, and let's just forget about this entire conversation." I gave her a tight hug just to show her some compassion.

"Okay, Ms. Sutton." She wiped her eyes, took a deep breath, and started to walk out with her head bowed.

I reached out to her. "Jeanine, remember this never happened. Keep your head up and game face on. You're my eyes and ears now, you have my undivided attention with any issues you have."

She stood up straight, shook her head as she closed her eyes, put on a smile, and walked out of my office.

Whew, crisis adverted! Whatever amount I have at home will have to be good faith until I receive all copies of that tape.

When Jeanine left the office I went straight to her desktop and opened the calendar with all my meetings. I scrolled back to that night and pulled the name of the restaurant I had dinner with Daniel. I dialed the number immediately. I didn't wait for the hostess to finish her greeting before I interrupted her. "Hello, this may seem strange, but I had dinner there a few nights ago and had dinner with Daniel Tatum. Do you remember?"

"I'm sorry, but I cannot say yes or no."

"There's no restrictions on you giving me that information." I tried to polite about it, but I wasn't going to go back and forth with her. "My name is Amanda Sutton, an attorney, and it's vital to an ongoing federal case that any information you have on Daniel Tatum be given.

Unless you want an investigation into your establishment you better pass the phone before you lose your job," I lied using my scare tactic.

"Please hold," I heard.

The soothing music played in my ear as my annoyance of it all built inside of me. Suddenly, the phone clicked. I didn't know if it disconnected or was I transferred. I waited for a few seconds then said, "Hello? Hello?"

"Hello, I'm the manager. How can I help you?"

"You have a patron named Daniel Tatum who is involved in a federal investigation. Any information you have—"

"First, if you are a lawyer you should already know if you do not have a subpoena issued by a federal judge I cannot and will not give you any information. As an exclusive restaurant with scheduled reservations only we have that right."

I paused in thought for a moment. Maybe I went about this the wrong way. Money always got people talking. "Don't be surprised when the investigation turns on you." I hung up the phone contemplating if it would be worth the money to try.

I glanced at the time on Jeanine's desktop. *Shit, I'm going to be late!* I hurried into my office to gather my files of my next client and rushed out the office. My mind was in a whirlwind of contemplations and deceptions. I could go down there and try my luck or push my weight around until I got what I wanted. If I used my connections then I would have to come up with a reason. Did I really want all that trouble? If I could settle this tonight would it be over?

26

Regina

Connie did as she was told and sent me Mark's calendar with all his meetings with Vanessa and some with other clients. I had to call a friend. I walked out my home with mixed feelings heading to Mark's meeting at noon. *Should I even pay attention to Vanessa's advances? I shouldn't be threatened by her, after all I have the ring! But a conniving bitch will always be persistent.* I had to get something on her.

The cab arrived in front of the building where Mark was showing a space. As of late I'd popped up on all his meetings with Vanessa like clockwork. He may not have liked it, but secretly I knew he wanted it. Knowing all the wrong I'd done to him it would be very easy for him to slip into her arms for revenge just to get back at me. I took a deep breath and entered the building not sure if my pop-ups would cause more drama than I wanted.

I called the elevator down and entered, pressing the PH button. When the elevator arrived at the floor as the doors opened a disheveled woman came close to knocking me down. "Excuse me!" She didn't bother to apologize; she smiled and adjusted her dress. At first sight of her face I didn't recognize her, but after the elevator doors closed it hit me. What the fuck was she doing here? She was the hostess at the party Tony took me to. Was my mind playing tricks on me? Was I right about Mark all along? My mind was flushed with confusion. I didn't know if I should just pretend I never saw her, or confront him like an insecure dummy.

I knocked on the open door. "Hello, Mark?" Mark appeared upset as he walked out one of the bedrooms. I knew it was the bedroom because I saw the floor plan to stage all the furniture. Why was he so upset? "Mark, is everything okay?"

"Yeah, yeah, what are you doing here?"

"I thought maybe I could grab some lunch with my future husband. Was that a new client?" I decided to keep everything to myself and let him tell it.

"No, it wasn't. Where do you want to go for lunch?"

I fought the urge to expand on the no and put on a smile. "There's that Korean grill spot not far from here."

"I'm good with that, let's go," he said with some kind of annoyance.

I didn't want to rock any boats because we were in a good place. We hailed a cab and went to the restaurant. We casually talked about the wedding during lunch, but I felt there was something he was holding back from me. I chose not to elaborate on what I was feeling so I kept my mouth shut. Maybe talking about our trip to the doctor would put him in a better mood.

"So, Mark, when are we going back to the doctor? I can't lie, I was amazed by all the scientific breakthroughs and to know so many people had children this way. I'm very excited."

He finally cracked a smile. "Yes, it's crazy isn't it? To have someone else carry our baby. I mean, our DNA, no one else's. Did you go through any of the potential surrogates' profiles?"

"I did, but I'm just not comfortable with a perfect stranger. Are you okay with that? I mean we won't know who she is, how she eats, who she hangs out with. Stuff like that matters. What if the person we pick looks good on paper, video, and over the phone, but maybe she's depressed for real?"

"Sounds like you're either having second thoughts or you have someone in mind." He pushed his plate forward.

He was still smiling so that was a good thing. "No and yes. No to second thoughts. Yes to the idea of someone we know. Honestly Mark, I don't think as an expectant mother I would be comfortable with our surrogate living apart from us. Is that crazy?"

"No, it's not crazy, but having her live with us is a little weird. A stranger having access to our inner sanctum," he said waving the waitress over for the check.

"Umm, I think you're forgetting the bigger picture, our baby. We can get a place out in California with some kind of extended space. Are you prepared to rent a house for an entire year? I know you mentioned getting something for six months, but—"

"Regina, whatever you want I'll make it happen. Now, I have to get back to the office for a meeting. Will you head back home or do you have to check on the building?"

"Actually, I'm going to try to meet up with Amanda. Hopefully she's available. See you later at home." I gave him a quick kiss on the lips before he walked out. I stayed seated at the table and pulled out my phone, scrolling through his calendar. *He doesn't have any other appointment. Why is he lying?* I dialed Amanda.

"Hey, chick, what's up? I'm on my way into a meeting."

"We have to talk. There are some serious situations I need advice on. When can we talk?"

"I can't today. I have a thing tonight. How does breakfast sound tomorrow?"

"Are you sure you can't stop by tonight? It's really important. Can't you reschedule your little booty call?" I was disappointed by her pushing me to the side.

"I can't, Regina. Listen I have to go. I will call you in the morning."

She hung up so fast I didn't get a chance to plead my urgency anymore. I tucked my phone back into my purse and left the restaurant. I wanted to head straight to Mark's office to see what he was up to, but decided on going home to finish up some paperwork on the new tenants who would moving into one of the buildings we owned.

It was six o'clock and Mark wasn't home yet. I decided on ordering in some Thai food. It was Mark's favorite. I had to make sure it was all perfect. Just then he walked through the door.

"Regina?" he shouted as he door shut.

"Hello, baby." I kissed him on the cheek.

"What's this? I thought we were going out for dinner." He placed his satchel onto the kitchen countertop.

I set the table and placed the food in serving plates. It was still warm. "I thought eating in would be better. It seemed as though your day wasn't going good when we met for lunch. Do you want to tell me what happened?" I didn't want to badger him with questions. I thought I would ease into it.

"What are you talking about?" I could feel the attitude building.

"I don't want to upset you. Why don't we just have dinner while the food's still warm? Here have a seat." I pulled out a chair, took a seat, and started to dish food onto the empty plates.

"Thai food?"

"Yes, it's your favorite."

"I know, and I also know if there's something on your mind we eat Thai food, especially if you're not certain of my reaction. So just go ahead and ask me." He shoveled food into his mouth.

"I'm going to ask Amanda to carry our baby," I said almost in a whisper.

He dropped his fork. His eyes widened. He stared at me as if I booked a one-way ticket to Mars for the both of us.

"Stop looking at me like that. It's not a bad idea."

"Regina, you are crazy. I'm not having her carry our baby. That's like having Satan carry our baby."

I was floored. I knew he didn't like her, but to think she's evil that was off the wall.

"She's not carrying our baby. She only cares about herself. She doesn't even have the instinct to be a mother. How could you even suggest that?"

"She's my best friend, Mark. It makes a lot of sense to me. I trust her. I don't trust those profiles. How is it so easy for you to pick a random stranger instead of someone who's close to me?"

He pushed his plate to the side. "Regina, if this is what you want"—he looked into my eyes—"I can't go through with it. Any of it."

I was crushed. Tears formed in my eyes. *Any of it? What is that supposed to mean? No marriage, no baby? What?*

"Mark, you can't be serious!" I said as tears rolled down my face. Had I now destroyed the only thing I ever wanted? "I thought you wanted all this. I thought you wanted me to be happy."

"I do want you happy, but that doesn't mean I have to just go with whatever you want. Yes, I want to marry you. Yes, I want to have our baby. She's not the one. How do you not see that?"

I was crying like a baby. He came over to me, pulled me up into his arms, and held me.

"I'm going to tell you something. It's going to be hard to accept it. But I need you to stop crying. Let me open a bottle of wine. Go to the bathroom, wipe your tears, and meet me in the bedroom, okay?"

My body went numb. What was he about to tell me? Was it about Amanda or that woman I bumped into today? I was scared, but open to what he had to say. I nodded my head yes and walked to the bathroom in our bedroom. When I entered the bathroom I closed the door and looked into the mirror wiping my eyes. "Listen to him. Don't react. He's the man you're going to spend the rest of your life with. Be the good woman you want to be," I said out loud and repeated in my mind when I walked out into the bedroom.

Mark was seated on the lounge in front of the fireplace with a look of defeat on his face. "Here." He held the glass to me. "Have a seat." His tone was upsetting.

"Mark, you're scaring me. You act as though you're about to tell me something awful. Please just spit it out!" My voice turned loud.

"Regina, know that I love you and will and have done everything for you. Amanda shouldn't be your friend or the woman carrying your baby."

"Mark, I know you and she don't get along, but she's very opinionated and she just doesn't see things from your prospective all the time. You can't be mad at her for having an opinion, she's a lawyer for Christ's sake." I laughed and moved closer to him.

His eyes were giving me a bad sign.

"Regina, I slept with Amanda long time ago."

My heart stopped beating. My world was crashing before my eyes. Was I hearing correctly? Did he just say he fucked my best friend?

"First, I knew her before you met her at that party. When you guys became friends I didn't want to ruin what we had over something that meant absolutely nothing. It happened once. That is why we never got along. I never wanted her in the house when I was around. You may not believe me, but she's your friend because she wants to be you. She's jealous of you, what you have, and the life you live. I'm sorry, I should have told you that night of the party. I'm sorry, Regina."

My head was spinning. My life was flashing before my eyes. *I finally decided on being the best woman I can be and he reveals this! What am I supposed to do now? All these plans, our future, is it over?*

"Regina, say something." He emptied his glass and poured another.

I couldn't. Words weren't forming. All I did was stare. Tears fell from my eyes.

"Regina, I don't feel anything for her. I never did."

After minutes of just staring and tears falling my hand reached to his face smacking him.

"I deserved that." He rubbed his face.

I said nothing. My hands were shaking. I put my glass down on the small side table.

"Regina, say something please." He grabbed my hand and squeezed it. "I can't lose you. I couldn't keep it from you anymore. When you asked for her to carry our child, there was no way I could move forward without telling you."

"I can't believe you. If it happened before me and her were friends, why didn't you just tell me then? It would have saved me a whole lot of heartache and pain. You know I don't have many real friends, and for you to look the other way when I allowed her into my life, our life, how can I forgive you? I don't care about the sex. It was once and never thought about again. But you kept it from me even after you saw me and her becoming closer."

"There's more, but before you start bashing me, which I deserve, you should know she's the one who told me you were seeing other men.

Not one man, but men. Think of how I felt when I heard that." He downed half his glass. "She still wants me and tries every chance you're not around."

What the fuck was happening? I didn't know how to respond to the bullshit he was trying to feed me, but could it be factual? *Listen to him. Don't react. He's the man you're going to spend the rest of your life with. Be the good woman you want to be.* I took a deep breath. There was only one person to set this all straight.

27

Tony

"Are you there yet?"

"No, just a little more."

I'd been thrusting in and out for the past forty minutes with my mind on Regina. It didn't matter who I was doing, my mind was solely on her. I watched her today. It took strength not to approach her. Not to hear her voice. Not to smell her scent. Not to touch her soft skin. She was serious about not seeing me anymore and I couldn't stand it.

"Are you there yet?" I asked again forcing myself to stay hard. I pumped harder with conviction. This wasn't a new client, but she was a paying top dollar for me to make her cum. I thought taking a client would get my mind off Regina, but it just reminded me of how much I needed her.

"Do you have to be somewhere?"

My dick went limp. I pulled out of her moist pot and removed the condom. I stood at the edge of the bed and tossed the condom in the garbage. *I should just apologize, pay for the room, and go the hell home!* I mulled over the backlash I would get and the money I would lose. Did it matter?

"Tony, are you okay?" she asked in her sweet tone.

"I'm sorry, it's not you. We can resched . . . Actually, I won't be available anymore. If you like I can refer you to someone. I'm really sorry." If giving up this life proved to Regina that I wasn't giving up on her then so be it. I had to start sometime.

"Refer me?" Her voice wasn't so sweet anymore. "I'm not going for that. I've paid you five grand every time we met for the past seven months. I've seen you no less than ten times. Now you want to take yourself off the market. I'm married, do you think I want to start this shit with someone new, again? Come on, Tony, I can't teach another young pup how, where, and when to touch to make me cum. Is it the money? I'll pay double the amount. Let's just chalk this up as a bad night on your part."

"Yes, let's do that. Don't worry about the room. I will take care of it."

"Are you asking me to leave right now?" She looked at me as if I had two heads.

"Yes." I walked into the bathroom, shut the door, and locked it. I didn't care anymore. I made my decision. There was no more of this. No more selling my body for the pleasures of other women. *I'm going to be the man she deserves.*

I opened the faucet to the shower and got in. I stood under the streaming hot water thinking of my future with the woman I was going to spend it with.

I arrived home greeted with a manila envelope shoved under my door. It brought a smile to my face. I knew what it contained. *Diana better have done a good job.* I needed this. I ripped the envelope open. I held my breath hoping it was good. I pulled out the pictures. *Yes, yes, this will work.* I took my phone out my pants pocket and dialed Diana.

"Hello?"

"Hey, Tony, I'm on my way to you now. Did I do what was needed?"

"It could have been better, but it'll work. It will have to work."

"You're still going to help me out tonight right?"

"I really don't think it will be a good idea. She knows what I look like and she's been causing a headache at my boy's restaurant."

"You have to or at least let me tell you what I'm doing."

"The tape should be enough to get what you want. I'll see what else you need to do."

"Open the door, I'm downstairs."

Diana had a problem with getting just enough; instead she fought for more and beyond. She caused more harm to herself because of her greediness. I buzzed the front entrance open and soon there was a knock at my door. I opened it and turned my attention back to the pictures of her and Mark.

"Hello." My back was turned to her as she stepped over the threshold.

"Hey," I answered still showing her my back.

She wrapped her arms around me and kissed at my neck. "What are you looking at?"

I showed her the pictures.

"Who is this guy to you?" She took the picture and pointed to Mark.

"No longer a problem from the looks of these pics. Thanks."

"So I guess I'm not the only one trying for a payday." She laughed.

I snatched the picture out her hand. "Unlike you, my goal is not money. It's a future with the woman I truly love."

Her face showed surprise from my words. "I hope you're not talking about the same woman you showed up at the event with. It seemed to me she had other plans and you were far from being included."

"Why don't you just shut up! You don't know anything."

"Oh, but I do. I know that every time she treats you as a toy or what you really are you seek me out. Is that the woman you want? I thought we were more than sex."

"You are no more to me than the bitches I fuck for money!" I was angry so I cut her with my words. Although, she was meaningful to me regardless of how I felt at this moment.

"Fuck you, Tony! You're a piece of shit! I'm trying to get this money for you and this is how you want to treat me. If this isn't some shit after you're the one putting me to shit to benefit your ass!"

"What are you trying to get at?" I wanted her to leave immediately. I wouldn't care if it was the last time I saw her. I didn't need her anymore.

"You think I'm stupid? Just some dumb, pretty chick you could manipulate. Hell, no! I knew from the start what you had in your mind." She paused with a smirk on her face. "Did you forget who approached you? Did you think it was because of your dick?" She belted a hearty laugh.

Now, I was confused. She had nothing on me. If she reported anything to anyone she would be held accountable too. All the info I had about clients was given to me by her.

"You're just as stupid as the dumb bitches who pay you to fuck them. I admit you were good, shit sometimes you were more than good, but trust me you're not the best. I think you forgot I never paid your ass for anything. That Web site shit you allowed me to take control of was only the start. You allowed me into your life. Tell me who else knows where you live? I mean what is this? Where the hell is all this shit coming from? For the past few months we've been seeing each other every other day. I thought we were more."

She was right. I'd been leading her on; making her my crutch for when Regina tucked me back into the closet. I dropped my head. "Listen, Diana, we helped each other. We used each other. Now, we just have to go our own way. There was never an 'us.' You must've known that."

Her body language changed. Her hands were on her hips. Her eyes filled with water fighting to bust through. She paced the floor, thinking of how to rebut the truth.

"Is that how you really feel? Just like that? I wish I could turn the switch as easy as you. I don't believe this. I may be giving up everything when I go meet Amanda tonight. As a friend, are you going to leave me hanging?"

Oh, my God! Really was she trying to tug on my sympathy strings? It didn't matter. I needed her gone. "Diana, we can't go on like this. This life is over for me. This—you, me—wasn't going to last forever. I'm not that guy. You had to have known that." Was she being naïve or just plain ol' dumb? I was beginning to lose my temper again.

Diana put her fingers under her eyes trying to push her waterworks back.

It was over. "I did you that one solid with Amanda. You shouldn't have any more problems with her. Just make sure you don't give her all the copies. I'm not going with you. I'm sorry, Diana, but you have to go."

She said nothing as she walked toward the door. Diana looked back to me with hurtful red eyes.

I just shook my head and turned my back to her. That was it. If I wanted a clean slate, I had one. Feeling bad for her was not a part of me. I gathered the pictures back into the envelope and pulled my phone out my pants pocket.

Regina need 2 see u. Important.

Minutes passed with no reply. I sent the same message to her Facebook, Twitter, and e-mail accounts. An hour had passed and I did everything under the sun to get a reaction from her, leaving messages starting off sweet, but with the more time passing it ended nasty each time.

Nothing.

I started to pace the floor and replay my options. Going over there at this moment wouldn't solve anything. It would only cause more hurt to Regina. Besides I would never be able to get past the doorman. She would hate me for displaying his so-called infidelity like a trophy. It would have to be private, by herself with no one in earshot or to interject their two cents. I took a breath and reached for a glass to pour a stiff drink.

After drinking one glass after the other of whiskey, I must've passed out on the sofa. I woke up the next morning feeling like shit. My stomach started to bubble, my mouth was building with saliva, and my head felt like a jackhammer was working on my skull. The rush of me standing up put me on auto spin like a washing machine. I threw up immediately all over myself and the sofa. There was no time to get to the bathroom. The smell alone made me empty whatever was left in my stomach again. "You stupid asshole! You know you had shit to handle today! Fuck!" I cursed at myself using my sleeved arm to wipe my mouth. I saw my phone on the floor with the indicator light blinking. "Oh shit," I said slowly easing myself to all fours to retrieve the phone.

When I picked up the phone and looked at the screen, there were five missed calls listed from Diana. I thought I'd made it clear to her that there was no reason to contact me. She left a couple of messages, but I didn't bother to listen to any. I erased them all. I swiped the screen checking all my social accounts hoping there was something from Regina. There was only my hope and foul-smelling breath responding to me. "Oh shit." I looked at the clock; it was almost seven. "Damn, I better clean up and get myself together." I had to get my head back into the game if this was going to work.

28

Amanda

It was almost ten when I got into the cab. Thank goodness no one knew I was carrying over $30,000 in cash tucked neatly into the front pocket of my satchel bag. I was nervous as hell. I suspected it would be Daniel meeting me. *Slimy dirt bag of a man, stooping lower than the shit on the ground to extort women. Don't worry, Mr. Daniel Tatum, I'm going to get you someway somehow.*

I exited the cab at the main entrance into Washington Square Park. It was late, but the summer night brought the college students to the dealers and swindlers of the community out to enjoy the night air. I stood under the arch scanning the groups of people. I didn't see him. I clutched my satchel tighter to my waist. I looked at my watch; it was five after ten.

People were walking their dogs, jogging through the park, sitting around the fountain, but he wasn't there. I walked into the park toward the fountain; that's when someone walking behind me touched my shoulder.

"Excuse me, do you have a light?" a familiar voice asked, coming from a dark hooded sweat suit.

"I don't smoke, sorry." I tilted my head to get a better look at the person asking.

The person stepped closer and pulled off the hood.

Diana?

"By the look on your face, I'm sure you expected someone else."

I was floored—a cluster fuck to the tenth power. Shit!

"Still nothing to say, okay I guess I can tell you the headline of tomorrow's news desk, highly reputable defense lawyer accused of rape and extortion. How does that sound?"

I laughed to relieve some of my nervousness. Diana looked at me with eyes of permanent hurt. She started to shake her leg and folded her hands across her chest: a sign of impatience and aggressiveness. This was not going to be easy. *Not having all the money may cause more harm than good,* my mind revealed.

"I guess I have your answer." She turned around and started to walk away.

I wanted to let her go, but I couldn't risk it. "Stop, Diana."

She halted and turned toward me. "Why should I? Weren't you ready to bring me down, pin me as some functional junky with a distorted past? All I wanted was the appropriate amount of monies due to me. Did you actually think when I found out who you really were I wasn't going to come at you? Don't be stupid. All I want is sixty grand and your dark little secret goes to the grave with me."

"So that guy works with you or is he your boyfriend who put you up to it? I hope he didn't come up with it."

"First, that wasn't my boyfriend."

Her expression changed; I felt some malice in her voice.

"He was just another dick being used for my purpose."

There was an opening to get this Daniel, I thought. It was time to plead my case. "Can we go somewhere and discuss this like two women instead of standing here like we're in search for a fix?" If she agreed, there was definitely a chance to come out on top.

She looked around the park, as did I, at the surrounding drug dealers staring at us, itching for a sale.

"Yeah, we can go down to the diner across from the West Fourth Street train station."

We walked the few blocks in silence. There was something that pissed her off about Daniel and I needed to know what it was.

When we entered the diner we walked to the farthest booth away from everyone. We waited for the waitress to hand us the menus. I ordered coffee for the both of us and shooed her away.

"Listen, I'm willing to pay you whatever price you put forth. I shouldn't have done what I did to you and quite honestly I never thought I would see you again. So when you approached me again, I was angered by your threats and demands, that's why I had all the ammo stacked against you."

"Look, Amanda, I'm not here to hear why you did what you did. I'm not stupid, you're a lawyer, and I know what you are up to. This is just a ploy to negotiate. What's your offer? Before I get up, walk out of here, and make your life a horrible mess."

I guessed she knew a little more than I thought! I smiled as the waitress strolled over with our coffee in hand. "Thank you," we said in unison.

I reached into my satchel and pulled out the neatly folded paper bag then placed it on the table. Diana seized the bag, opened it under the table, and shook it back and forth.

"This is not sixty. More like half, if that. Do you really think I'm joking? Did you not get the message when I sent that video to your secretary? Okay, I'll just have to—"

"It's thirty only because I was in court most of the day and couldn't get to the bank. You will have the rest tomorrow morning."

"Fine, but if I don't have the rest in the morning before ten, court or no court, your embarrassment will be ten times more. I swear on everything I love." She sipped her coffee.

"I understand. We both know I don't want any of that footage out. I'm a great defense lawyer, but you know the saying, 'a man who is his own lawyer has a fool for a client.' Besides there's no way to deny footage. I just have one request."

"And that is?"

"All copies of it. Since you sent the little snippet via e-mail, I trust you have a flash drive with the entire video."

"As soon as I receive all my money, I will gift wrap it for you."

"That's not all. I want Daniel."

She laughed almost spitting her coffee on me. "Do you plan on prosecuting him? Or fucking him?"

"Maybe both, what is it to you? He's nothing to you, right? Why would you care if I use him for my purpose now?"

She sat back and sipped on her coffee a little more before saying anything.

"First his name is not Daniel. It's Tony and he can be easily bought for a fee. I think his going rate is five grand."

I didn't know how to digest her statement. Did I really get conned by a gigolo?

"He's what I call a ladies' man, but I think his lifestyle has changed."

"And what does that mean?"

"He broke the one rule of the handbook: he fell in love with his own client. A married one at that. There's no coming back from that."

By her tone, I could tell she was heartbroken. "Were you a client?"

She cut her eyes at me. "Hell no!" I saw the waitress look over to us.

I touched a nerve.

"That's it with the interrogation. Just have my money tomorrow." She got up from the booth and stuffed the brown paper bag in her purse.

"I'll pay you an extra twenty grand to put him in front of me."

She laughed. "Oh, so now I work for you? I don't think so. You want him, get your detective to look him up. Good luck."

"Let's make it another forty, then. Are you really going to pass on something that takes no effort? I just said you had to put him in front me. I'm sure that will come easy to you, no?" I baited her, hoping to ignite her resentment against him.

"Get me my money." She walked out the diner without another word.

I pulled out my phone and swiped the screen.

"Amanda, what's up?"

"Steve, I have a job for you, but it's a bit personal."

"You know how I feel about personal shit."

"Yeah, I know. Double the fee with a bonus for your confidentiality." I sighed.

"Personal is my specialty. Send me what you need and give me a few days. Whatever it is you'll get. Is that it?"

"Yes, I'll send it to you once I'm home. I need you on this right away. Good night."

I hung up feeling confident he'd get me what I needed to tie this Tony up so he'd be begging for my help. I called the waitress over to pay the check.

As soon as I stepped out the diner my phone rang, Regina displayed on the screen. "Hey, girl, wha—"

"You dirty fucking bitch! You slept with Mark and then befriended me. You sly, sneaky bitch!

Were you friends with me just to be close to him? Did you tell him all that I told you thinking he would leave me for you?" She was on ten.

"What in the hell is going on?"

"Shut the fuck up, you nasty, sneaky little bitch! I never want to see your ass again! If we happen to see each other out somewhere, you better hope I don't embarrass your ass. Or, better yet, stoop to your level and beat the shit out of you."

"Regina, can you just calm down for a second and explain to me what the fuck is going on?" I never heard her talk to me with such hate and disgust. What the fuck was really going on?

"You heard me, bitch!" The phone clicked in my ear. I rushed to call her back, but pushed End as soon as it rang.

My entire body shook. I stood there staring into nothing holding my phone, wondering if I should call Mark. Calling him would only make things worse. *What makes her think she can talk to me like that? She just pissed off the wrong one. If she wants to see a bitch, I can show her how much of a real bitch I can be. I think it's time Regina finds out I'll be in their lives forever whether she wants it or not. The real shit is about to hit the fan!*

29

Tony

After cleaning up and a couple hours of much-needed sleep to rid the hangover feeling, I was ready—ready to confront Regina. I thought about calling, but I didn't. Instead I called Mark's office. "Hello, is Mark Sands in today?"

"Yes, may I—"

I touched End on the screen before the female voice could finish her question. I knew from watching Regina, once he was in the office he wouldn't be home until after five, sometimes six. I grabbed the envelope with the pictures and headed to Regina's.

When the cab turned on to York Avenue I made him stop a block away from her building. I got out and walked toward her building on the opposite side of the street. I stood in front of a small newspaper stand and watched the front of her building for any signs of her. It was a little after one in the afternoon. The envelope was tucked under my right armpit.

Fifteen minutes passed. It was time.

I walked to the building.

"Hello, sir," the doorman greeted me.

"Yes, I'm here to see Regina Clay," I said reaching into my pocket.

"Let me buzz her," he said picking up the phone.

I placed my hand on the phone with a hundred dollar bill. It was awhile since I'd stepped into this building and usually Regina would have already set it up to allow me in through the service entrance.

"Sir?"

"Listen, I'm a friend of hers. I want to surprise her. I haven't seen her in a very long time and I don't want Mark to know I've seen her. It's a down low thing." I winked. I prayed he would fall for it. I was sure he could use the extra money. I dropped another hundred dollar bill on the phone. "I promise, I'm no stalker or anything like that. Trust me."

He snatched the bills and slid them into his pocket. "Go on up."

I stepped onto the elevator and pushed the top floor button on the panel. It'd been a long time since I entered her building. Everything was so pristine. I missed this place. The lobby had fresh flowers perched on tables, hanging art on the walls, the elevator smelled of wood oil that was recently applied, and when the doors opened to my desired floor a floral scent hit my nose with full force. There were flowers layered along the hallway on ledges against the wall. It smelled good, but was just too much for me. I looked to the right then the left. There were two. Shit, which door was it? I walked down the hallway slowly, trying to listen for Regina's voice.

Fuck it! I walked up to the first door closest to me and knocked.

The door opened and there she was, beautiful as the day I met her.

"What the fuck are you doing here, Tony?"

"Regina." I smiled.

"I'm calling the cops!"

She tried to shut the door, but I stuck my foot out to stop it from closing and rushed inside. "Regina, please I just want you to listen to me. I promise I will leave, just please listen to me. I'm not here to hurt you."

Regina stopped and turned around. "What are you doing here, Tony? What do you want?"

"Regina, I love you. I need to—"

She threw her hands in the air annoyed. "Tony, we've been through this. I'm not leaving Mark and you better hurry with whatever you have to say because he will be home soon."

Why was she lying? I opened the envelope and placed the pictures on the kitchen countertop. "Please look," I whispered. I had to play this to the best of my abilities.

Regina eyes widened and her jaw dropped.

"Regina, he's not the one. He doesn't really love you. This is not the only one. After you stopped seeing me, I didn't know what else to do. I had to prove to you we could work. I've cut off all ties with all my clients. I no longer have that phone, that life is gone."

"How did you get these pictures?" Her voice whimpered as she shuffled through all the pictures.

"I didn't want to tell you before I knew for sure. I had him followed. Please I'm not lying. Do you really want him? Your connection to him left when you started fucking me. You know our relationship was real. Something we both needed. You needed my affection, my unconditional love, my undivided attention without anything in return. You gave me the chance to love again. It wasn't the sex. You already knew sex wasn't anything I was lacking."

She said nothing. Her eyes were still scanning the pictures.

I stepped closer to her, putting my arms around her. Her scent was intoxicating. "Please believe me. I don't want you to get hurt by him. Please say something," I spoke into her ear.

She pushed me back. "Get the fuck out of here! Why would you do this to me? This is the man I'm about to marry. We're going to start a family. Why are you doing this?"

A family? What was she talking about? She couldn't have kids.

"Are you trying to destroy me? Tony, you can't provide for me. You don't even own your apartment. How could you provide as a man should when you don't even have a job? Fucking sex-deprived women is not a career! Get the fuck out my house! I don't ever want to see you again!"

Was she really kicking me out after seeing those pictures? "Regina, don't be so naïve." I stepped closer.

She pushed me back again and reached for her phone. "If you don't get the hell out of my house I'm calling the cops. Trust me, it'll be very easy to convince them that you hit me. How many felonies do you have? Or maybe I should make a call to the IRS. I wonder if that would hurt your little cash-funded lifestyle." She swiped her screen, threatening to push Send on the 911 display.

I walked to the front door hoping she would stop me for any reason. I was walking away without her, for now, but soon she would be mine. I promised myself. I unwillingly left her building wishing like everything she was walking out with me.

By the time I returned home, my perfectly planned future went up in flames. I was sure the pictures would shed some light and she would easily fall into my arms. How could I've been so wrong?

30

Vanessa

I walked into my office feeling like shit. My wild night of drinking tequila and snorting coke was slowly creeping up on me. I entered my private bathroom and pulled out a small bottle with the white substance inside. I took a couple of bumps just to put my head back in order. As soon as I walked out rubbing my nose, Charles greeted me.

"So we're back to that stage again, huh?"

"Why are you in my office?" I rolled my eyes.

"Look at yourself!" He closed my office door and took a seat.

I already knew the speech; we'd been down this road before.

"Look at yourself, you're a mess and your mess is affecting the business our parents built. I can't have you working here like this anymore.

You need to go back to rehab. I've made all the arrangements, there's a car downstairs waiting for you," he insisted.

"Fuck you, Charles! I'm not going!" I shouted.

"Listen, I wouldn't be doing this if I didn't love you. You have two choices: either you take my help and get on the straight path, or you can continue your ways until you demolish your very existence and everyone who loves you."

"You're not the boss of me! Get out of my office!" At this point I was livid with his dismissal of my feelings of how I live my life.

"You need to stop. Stop everything. I know what you've been doing to Mark. You don't have to ruin another marriage with your slutty ways! Leave him alone! All his future endeavors with this company will go through me, no one else. He's made me aware of all the late nights where you tried to force yourself onto him and God knows what you said to his wife!"

"She's not his wife!"

"She may not be his wife, but she's more than you'll ever be to him. I'm not trying to make this harder for you or put ourselves into another binding lawsuit because you can't act appropriately. You're going to rehab so you shouldn't be a problem to him or me anymore."

"A problem? Is that what I am, Charles? A problem?"

"You've always been a problem, Vanessa. You and I both know that."

"Maybe I should solve the problem for everyone. I bet you would love that, right?" I threatened.

"Really? I never said a word to you when you left our father facing death because of your selfish reasoning on breaking up a marriage of one of his good friends. I never mentioned it to any one of our siblings to save you from being blamed and hated. I covered your ass and swept it all under the rug. Now, I refuse to continue to be like Dad with fixing your wrongs. Dad always saw the good in you and you left him there to die!"

His words hurt. I stayed silent wanting it to all stop permanently. There was no hope of being the little sister I once was. He made it clear; love was destroyed, once again, by my selfish ways. There was nothing I could do about it, but accept it.

"After rehab, you should go elsewhere. Don't come back here. You only cause devastation and destruction. I can't partake in your self-destruction."

"I'm sure Mom is not having any of this. Your ego has always been your biggest rival and she knows that. Let's give her a call," I warned hoping it would shake him.

"She agrees and respects my decision as the sole owner of this company."

"What the fuck are you talking about?" I was confused momentarily.

"She signed over the entire company to me. You have no stake in this anymore." He waved his hands around the office.

"You can't do this to me. I built this just as much as you did. I deserve my share whether you like it or not," I demanded.

"I agree. Once you've completed rehab and attend regularly scheduled meetings you will receive an allowance to do as you wish. You can decide on where you'll live, I will make sure the rent will be paid for the entire year. After that you will be on your own. If you decide to go back to your old ways, there will be no support of any kind." He was serious this time.

"So, are you telling me I'm going to be put to the side like trash for something I can't control? All because of my addictions?

"Addictions? For now, yes, until you can prove to us that you'll never be the careless wreck you once were. When you're ready security will escort you downstairs. Everything is packed and ready for you in the car."

"I'm your blood, Charles! You can't do this to me!" I screamed.

"I can and I will, Vanessa." He left my office without another word.

Fuck him! He can't do this to me! He doesn't own me! He can't cut me out the family! Fuck him and what he wanted me to do. I wasn't ready for rehab again!

I had to get out of the office without him knowing. Charles left the door wide open so I saw he was telling the receptionist something. I knew for a fact he wouldn't let her in on family business so when he made his exit so did I. Grabbing my purse off the chair, I walked out with my head held high. When I was about to pass the reception area, the receptionist called out to me.

"Excuse me, Ms. Shore, should I call security to help you to the car?"

"Amy, it's okay. I'll be right back. I just have to run next door to the bank quickly," I lied.

"Are you sure? Mr. Shore—"

"Amy, I don't care what Mr. Shore had to say. Just like you're an adult, so am I." I put her in her place. As I made my exit out to the elevator, I could see her reaching for the phone. I pushed on the elevator button, but decided taking the stairs would get me out the building faster.

I had to talk to Mark. Because of him I'd now been ousted by my own family. That motherfucker wouldn't be telling lies on me. He knew his ass would have taken it if his girlfriend wasn't on to my game.

31

Mark

My head was pounding a mile a minute, heading out the door. I hated leaving Regina this morning. Our conversation was the first I'd ever felt was actually real. Something I'd always wanted. She never talked to me unless it was about something she needed done: new house, new business ventures, and the next dinner party we had to have. It became a routine we fell into. Nothing of substance between us, more like a business relationship. We lost that aspect of us—the love, the respect, and most of all the communication.

If I didn't have such a huge meeting this morning I would have pushed back any- and everything. *I should have though,* came into my mind as I reached my morning meeting. *I'll call her once I get into the office.* I stepped into the meeting with only Regina on my mind.

Regina's truth scared me. I didn't realize we both fell out of love. For years, I believed it was just me. I didn't know her need for sex was so different from mine. There were months where having sex was not my priority, it was affording her the lifestyle she wanted, we both wanted. The need for a family was all me; having kids was never in her future. I realized forcing her to go through the procedure with a total stranger was selfish. Yes, I wanted kids, but if she wasn't ready I had no right to force it on her. When she opened my eyes to the extortion I was putting forth before her, why wouldn't she resent me in years to come? We had time and if she was never ready I'd be okay with that. Marrying her was the next step and stepping up to do so wouldn't make me any less of a man.

I stepped out the building and hailed a cab. After telling the driver where to go, my phone rang. I was expecting this call.

"Mark, I received the final deal. Well done," Charles said.

"Thank you, I hope you didn't have any doubt that I would get the job done," I said smirking.

"Mark, I have to have you on my team. I can't worry about cost. Whatever you want, I mean it!" he voiced with excitement.

I had to speak carefully. "Mr. Shore—"

"Charles, please," he insisted.

"Charles, I respect you and what your family has built. I strive for that every day. But I have to be honest with you, dealing with your sister has been challenging. Don't get me wrong I appreciate her even setting up our meeting. If it weren't for her I probably would be still trying to get a meeting." I waited for him to mull over my words.

"I'm sorry, that's my fault and I hope you don't hold it against me. She's had a lot of problems in the past and honestly I never have her on the front line so to speak. Vanessa is usually behind a desk and when she insisted on me meeting you I thought it was her way of proving to me that she was making an effort."

"I see. Umm . . . so you know about, umm . . ." I was struggling to tell him his sister was trying to get into my pants in the worst way.

"Mark, no need to go any further. I know how she is, after all she is my sister. There's one thing my father always told me: you can't choose your family. I know her ways and I can't let her ruin a budding business venture we're about have."

Damn, wasn't he confident! "Charles, I can't work with Vanessa and if she's going to be a part if this venture I will have to politely step away."

"Look, Mark, list your conditions. I can't afford for you to go elsewhere. We are about to buy a list of land that will probably bring your net worth up a few zeros."

"Land where?" This could be the bump my career needed to go abroad.

"On all continents. Everywhere, even Antarctica. Don't worry you won't have to sell there, it's just in the listing. But there is the global warming effect happening so we're ahead of the game." He laughed.

He wasn't joking though. I already knew the company was researching land everywhere. Now that I knew he in fact had the deal it would be stupid of me to let this opportunity pass on by. "Charles, there's no list of conditions. Working with your marketing team was impeccable and smooth. There's really only one condition, I'm not working with or for Vanessa. I strictly deal with you when it comes down to it. She's caused a few misconceptions in my household and moving forward that can no longer happen, even the possibility."

"Mark, I'm fine with that. There will no reason for her to contact you for anything. When can we sit down and work out the details with numbers? I'm free when you are."

"I'm taking care of some personal matters for the rest of the week, but I'll have Connie call your secretary and set up something for us."

"Sounds good. I look forward to it. Mark, if Vanessa attempts to call or see you, please ignore her respectfully and call me directly."

"Sure will, Charles."

"Oh and, Mark, I've already wired your bonus to the assigned accounts. But I would like to throw in something else. I guess when we meet I'll present it to you. You deserve it. I'll see you soon."

"Okay, see you then. Thanks again, Charles." As much as I should have been jumping for joy and doing cartwheels, I felt nothing. The cab arrived at the downtown building. I paid the driver and got out. I tried to shake it all off as I entered the building. Usually, when I walked into a conference room I had a clear mind; it prevented me from making rash decisions. Today wasn't that day.

After the meeting my head was still clouded with thoughts of Regina. I opted on not going to lunch offered and headed to my office to drop off some paperwork. "Good afternoon, Connie." I headed straight into my office.

"Ummm, Mr. Sands, Ms. Shor—" Her footsteps were right on my heels.

I opened my office door and there stood the unexpected Ms. Vanessa Shore. After the night I had, I sure as hell didn't need her shit piled on top.

"Ms. Shore, you're not supposed to be here. I have a very hectic schedule and can't deal with your shit!" I rested my briefcase on the lounge chair and took a seat behind my desk. I didn't bother to make eye contact because I knew she had ulterior motives.

"Connie, I'm good for now. I'll let you know if I change my mind, thanks," said Vanessa.

I heard the door shut. *Damn, here we go . . .*

"Good afternoon, Mark, I hope your day is going well."

"Vanessa, I have to meet a client in about an hour. I'm trying not to be as rude as you when you shut the door on Connie, but you need to leave. We have no business together."

"Mark, you know I wasn't being rude, just making sure she knew her place."

"If you say so." I arched my brow.

She reached into her large bag and pulled out a manila envelope. "I wanted to keep my end of the bargain." She held the envelope in the air like a prize. "It was your bonus."

I moved my chair to put some distance between us. "Thanks, but no thanks. Your brother already provided me with a bonus to my liking."

Vanessa wasn't used to hearing no. "Really, is that a fact? Did he give you extra for the bullshit you fed him, too?" she asked.

What the hell did she mean by that? Not once had I given her the impression I would take her up on her offer. I got up and walked around my desk to prevent her from pouncing on me like a wild attack dog in heat. "Vanessa, does your brother know you're here?" I hoped that scared her.

"My brother is not my keeper. My father is dead, that doesn't give my brother any authority over my life."

She tried to move closer to me, but I kept an object between us.

"Mark, stop fighting me."

She plopped down in the seat on the chair in front of my desk tired of my rejection probably. I had a gut feeling she was about to do something drastic. Finally, I felt better with her seated and the desk between us. "Vanessa, we have been through this before. I don't want anything with you. We have no business with each other. I deal with your brother Charles only. I've already spoken to him and he's willing to make sure you have nothing to do with me to secure any future business with me."

Her face turned red and her eyes burned into me. "Yeah, and where did that get you? Because it's pretty obvious he isn't doing shit to stop me from showing up."

She opened her crossed legs exposing her hairless flower. I closed my eyes.

"Vanessa, please leave." Was she losing her mind? Did she really think I would fall for her shit?

"Mark, you know you want this. You know if it weren't for me, you wouldn't have ever gotten that meeting," she said seductively as she rested one foot on the top of my desk causing her tight dress to inch up her thigh. She licked two fingers and started to rub her growing clit. "Mark, it will be between you and me. I can help you get a bigger piece of the pie."

I picked up the phone and hit the intercom button. "Connie, please call Charles Shore on his private number and let him know his sister is here. Thanks."

"Mark, don't you want to watch me cum? Ahhh . . . I know you want to."

I stood up and walked to the door. "Vanessa, you need help, seriously." I left her sitting there with the door wide open. She quickly ceased her seduction.

"Mr. Sands, Mr. Shore apologizes and says he'll handle it," Connie said with a confused look.

"Thank you, Connie. I'll be in the conference room. If Ms. Shore doesn't remove herself in less than five minutes call security."

"Mr. Sands, security?"

"Yes, immediately," I said with a stern tone.

"Okay, should I call—"

Just then I saw Amanda approach the main entrance to my office. "Connie, cancel the rest of my day. I'm going home."

"But, Mr. Sands, your next client is only here for a couple of hours before he heads back to Europe. I won't be able to reschedule for another week."

"Connie, if we have to Skype then so be it. But I'm not doing anything else today. Right now I have to handle some personal matters." I didn't bother to get my briefcase. I headed straight for the door.

"Mark—"

I grabbed her by her arm. "Not here. You have some serious explaining to do. Let's go!"

She yanked her arm away and stepped back. "Get your hands off of me!"

"Let's go!" I demanded again, this time pointing to the elevator.

"And where are we going?"

At the same time Vanessa walked out the office into our heated exchange of words. "Is this why you won't do me? Because you already had someone on the side? She's not much." Vanessa smiled looking at Amanda up and down. She pushed the button for the elevator and pulled at her dress.

"Who the fuck are you?" Amanda fed into her stupidity.

"I'm the one he really wants to fuck, but now will never get the chance since I'm face to face with you." She looked to me. "Have a good life, Mark, and hope your wife doesn't know about her. She would feel horrible to know you're fucking someone way below her."

The elevator doors opened and I thanked the heavens that her ass was gone once and for all. I had told Regina all about her efforts to get me in bed and in turn she told me about their little conversation at that impromptu luncheon. So whatever lies she might run to tell Regina, it would be a great laugh when Regina told me.

Amanda looked at me with folded arms across her chest and her foot tapping on the floor. "Is there something I need to know?"

"Can we please just leave the building? This is my place of business and I'd rather not have this conversation here." I pushed the button for the elevator.

"And who told you I want to go anywhere with you?"

"Amanda, we need to talk, all of us."

"All of us? Who is all of us?"

Was she confused or playing dumb?

The elevator doors opened and I stepped in motioning for her to join in. She rolled her eyes and with much hesitation walked in. On the ride down there was complete silence. We finally got out the building and I was relieved.

Amanda waited until we were farther from the building before saying what was on her mind. "I got a call from Regina last night cursing my ass out. What the fuck did you spill? I tried calling her, but she refuses to pick up."

"Regina knows everything about us."

"Everything? Like what? There's nothing here as you say."

"Everything. You being her friend only to get closer to me to us having the one-night stand."

Her eyes rolled so far back I thought she was about to faint. "Okay so, basically as of this moment my friendship with you guys is over, huh?"

"Yes." There was no need to sugarcoat anything with her now.

"I think we should all talk together. There's a few things I have to get off my chest concerning you two."

I was confused. What more could she have to say to Regina? If I were her I would be so embarrassed to show my face. "Okay, let me call her and see if she's up to it."

"Mark, be a man. Have some fucking balls. Why must you check with her? What I have to say concerns both of you and you both need to hear it."

I left my phone in my pants pocket and hailed a cab. The silence on the short drive to the condo was definitely uneasy. I racked my brain to figure out what she possibly would have to say after Regina cursed her ass out. Was she going to beg for our forgiveness? Was she going to come clean with everything or lie through her teeth?

32

Regina

I stared at the pictures Tony left on the counter. After all we talked about why wouldn't he tell me this? Was it true? I couldn't believe it, but these pictures before me told me an entirely different story. A picture speaks a thousand words as they say. *Should I call him? No, warning him would be a mistake. I need to see his face, which will tell me if he's lying.*

I looked at my phone. The light was blinking alerting me that I had a new message. When I picked it up, the screen read 3 Missed Calls, 3 New Voicemails, all from Amanda. Did she not understand when I told her I never wanted to speak to her again? I threw my phone on the sofa secretly hoping it would miss and break into pieces somehow. I heard the front door open.

"Regina," Mark's voice called out.

I heard two sets of footsteps on the marble tiled floor. *Who the hell?* "Why in the world would you bring this whore into our house?"

"Regina, there's no need—" Amanda tried to plead her reasoning to be in my house.

"There's no need for what? For a whore such as yourself to be in my house? Or, is this where you both tell me you're going to walk away together? Tell me Mark," I shouted.

"Regina, please. I knew her being here would upset you, but there's something she wants to tell both of us. Let's just hear her out and then she can leave without another word to us. Please." He walked toward me reaching for my hand.

"What could she possibly have to say to the both of us? She's a sneaky-ass, low-down, dirty bitch! You fell for her bullshit. She's just here to admire her work, you stupid fuck!" I snapped at him.

"Are you just going to call me names and think it's okay? If anyone of us is a dirty, sneaky bitch, it would be you!" Amanda opened her pathetic mouth.

She stepped closer. My hands weren't quick enough to gather the pictures on the counter. She snatched one and laughed.

"Oh, so you're aware that I wasn't the only one, huh?"

"What the . . ." Mark snatched the picture out of her hand. "What . . . Who . . . How . . ." He bowed his head as if he was caught and ashamed that his darkness came into the light.

"Oh, so it's true?" I threw all the pictures at him.

"This is not what it looks like, Regina. I promise you on everything I love." Tears came to his eyes.

"Oh, Mark, tears isn't going to get you out of this one!" By the sound of Amanda's laughter, she knew more than I did.

"Of course you would be enjoying this!" I looked to Amanda. "There's nothing more you would want than for me and Mark not to be together."

She laughed.

This was far from funny.

"Shut the fuck up, Amanda!" Mark surprised me with his defiance. "This is enough! There was nothing between us, nor will there ever be, especially after all this shit. I only tolerated you because of Regina and now since there's nothing between you two I'm cutting any ties you thought you had with me. You should leave. Whatever you needed to say can go to the grave with you because I don't give a fuck!"

Mark wasn't holding back with his tongue lashing, but it still didn't get him out of his wrong. I still believed Amanda knew more about those pictures.

"Oh stop it, Mark, you can't grow balls overnight! Regina, maybe you should ask Mark how he got himself in that predicament or maybe you should ask him who was at his office this afternoon. Mark, shall you share?" She boldly took a seat at the kitchen counter before picking up a photo off the floor.

My eyes burned into Mark waiting for his response. Was that woman at his office?

"First, don't you dare imply that those pictures were anything! Second, who was at my office is no concern of yours. Regina knows all about her."

"Mark, if those pictures aren't anything then why wouldn't you let Regina in on it? Regina, if you believe him you're better than me. I don't know for the life of me why I was so jealous of this relationship." She threw her hands in the air as if to say she didn't care.

"You wanted it on one occasion, isn't that why you told me about all the shit Regina was doing behind my back?" he shot back.

Shit, I didn't want anything to be turned on to me!

"Did she tell you everything about her infidelities? Or did she just tell you what you wanted to hear? Regina, did you let him know about the sex parties or the guy you were seeing for a year?"

"Why are you here?" I shouted.

"Amanda, you should leave before I call the cops," Mark spat at her.

"You're just a conniving little bitch aren't you? You want to destroy all what I have, don't you? Are you that jealous still? Should we get a restraining order against you to keep you out our lives? Are you that disappointed your ploy to break us apart didn't work?"

"Out your lives? Oh no, I will never be out your lives. It's the very reason why I'm here. I don't care that Mark will stay with you even if she's been fucking every Tom, Dick, and Harry. I don't care if he doesn't declare all his illustrious affairs. You guys are perfect for each other."

"What the hell is she talking about, Mark?" I demanded.

"Oh, I bet the woman in the picture could tell you all about it. I'll let you in on something: the woman in the picture probably did set up your husband. I can't say for sure, but you may want to ask your lover, Tony."

Was she really doing this to me?

"Tony? What does he have to do with these?" I snatched the picture out her hand.

"Who's Tony?" Mark asked confused.

I avoided his question and looked to Amanda for her response.

"Oh, I guess I will have to share this information since Regina feels the need to ignore your question. Tony was one of the men she's been fucking, except their connection has been on for a year maybe even longer. You see, I've been put in a situation where I had to look into a few things."

"You know nothing of what you're saying or that woman in the picture. Just leave, Amanda, you can't play tricks on us anymore!" Mark stood before her pointing to the door.

"Mark, I'm sure you didn't know Tony was fucking Regina in your very own bed."

"What! Amanda, if you don't get the fuck out my house I swear my hands will make you leave!" I had to threaten her.

"Regina, is she saying the truth? Tell me, were you fucking other men in our bed?"

"She was sharing the sheets all right with all who would. Regina, why lie now? Don't both of you have everything out on the table?"

She was pushing for something and it wasn't just a breakup between me and Mark. Amanda was out to destroy everything I had.

"Mark, why would you believe anything that comes out of her mouth right now? She has been denied her desperate chance to have you. Her entire dream has just turned to shit. Please, Mark, have some sense." I hoped my words took heed.

I saw her reaching into her bag. She pulled out a folder and placed it on the counter. I was tired of her hidden agendas.

"What's that, Amanda? Something you dug up or made up to give you an edge? Or let me guess some more pictures?" I taunted her.

She stood up as if her stance was something to fear. "Oh no, Regina, this is my permanent pass to contact your man whenever I feel fit. Consider yourself served." She waited for the look on our faces.

I wished she would die five times over after trying her almighty best to destroy my life. Mark rushed to the folder she neatly left on the counter. I was infuriated with him for bringing her into our home. How could he not see her real motives? All she wanted to do was hurt me because she couldn't have Mark. The shock was apparent on Mark's face.

"What is it, Mark, another one of her lies?"

He said nothing. His face was blank. His hands trembled as he picked up the folder.

"Mark?" I looked to Amanda's smug grin on her face. "What the fuck is that, Amanda?"

"I have a son."

My mouth dropped opened and I took the folder out his hand. There was a birth certificate, a picture of a toddler, and a court order for a DNA test along with a family court hearing date scheduled in two days.

This couldn't be. This couldn't possibly be true.

I looked to Mark and by his tears this was the start of an unwanted lifetime sentence we were both facing.

"Mark could this be true?" I hated to ask the question.

"Of course it's true, Regina."

I couldn't hold back any longer. My open hand hit her face with power.

"Regina." Mark jumped between us. "Regina, you're better than that, don't stoop to her level." He grabbed my hand.

His eyes showed the shame of it all. There were more truths to our relationship than what I was led to believe. I could only blame him for this ambush. There was a decision to be made: should I stay or should I go? Could I be the woman I intended to be for him?

"You are absolutely right, Mark. Stooping to her low level only shows her true character. I love you and we will get through this together." I turned to Amanda. "You, on the other hand, have some fucking nerve to play these games."

"Oh, it's no game, Regina, trust me." She rubbed the right side of her face.

"Fine, if he is proven to be the father then by all means he will be there for his son. I'm not vindictive like you to keep him away from some of the most precious moments of his son's life. He will be there and we will both see you in court. Now, it's time for you to leave."

"Oh, I'm going to make sure he's there whether he wants it or not."

Her smirk was getting on my very last nerve. I clenched my fist, but didn't swing at her. I counted in my mind to ten.

"Amanda, you need to leave before I have to call the cops to remove you. You've done all you had to here," I calmly remarked.

"Please call the cops so I can report your assault on me. You forgot your actions and words will be held against you."

"Amanda, please go!"

After a quick stare down she finally left us to deal with the reality we faced. Mark slammed the door behind her.

I walked over to the counter and picked up the folder. "Could this be a forgery? She is a lawyer. She could get her hands on these documents at any time. I don't see a raised seal of any kind."

"I don't know, Regina. I don't know." He took a seat with a pitiful look of defeat on his face.

"What's the matter with you? Stop this. Listen, we can call our lawyer right now to authenticate all this. Don't look like a lost puppy. If this is some trickery she's pulling, then we'll take action to the fullest extent of the law. I'm sure the district attorney would like to know how she came up with these documents."

I wanted nothing more than to believe this was all some elaborate scheme of hers that went too far, but remembering her smug grin made me think it was true. There was nothing I could do to make it all go away. Instead, I decided coming totally clean about Tony would make this situation much easier somehow.

"Mark, let's sit down, forget about all this for the moment. I will call the lawyer and we will find out if this is for real." I walked over to the sofa.

"Regina, I don't know what to say. My emotions right now are many," he said walking over to me.

"Come on, Mark, we have to talk this out. First, yes, it is true about Tony. I was seeing him off and on for over a year. I stopped seeing him completely a few months back. I want to marry you and grow old with you. Someone like that can only satisfy me one way. He has no substance, no ambition, he's not capable of being a true man. When I realized he was not able to provide me the comfort or security that you've shown me for the past eight years I ended it for good."

"So you were going to leave me?"

I had to be honest not only to him, but myself. "Yes, at one point. A lot has changed now, and I'm willing to work out all our issues including winning back your trust. I love you, Mark, and I refuse to allow Amanda or anyone to tear us apart."

"I can't understand why you would bring someone else into our bed. That's our place, our sanctuary, our—"

It brought tears to my eyes, thinking back on how much disrespect I displayed all for my pleasure. "I know, Mark, it makes me sick just thinking about it."

"I built this place all for you, Regina. Now I can't even imagine where else you and whoever must've done in this house."

"We can sell it. Buy an actual house with a backyard. We can leave right now. Let's go. I'll pack . . . No, I won't pack anything. Let's just start all over. Back to where we were, when we looked into each other's eyes all we would see was our love."

"So I'm supposed to forget all of this? Forgive you so easily? Would you?"

"Mark, I can't force you to forgive me, and I can't say I don't want you to forget. Shit, I want to forget! But if you still want me in your life, I won't deny you. Please, Mark, I love you."

"I need some time to think. I'm going to a hotel." He got up and walked to the door.

I understood this was enough to drive any good man away, but I had faith we would work through all of this. "Okay, Mark, I want to stop you, but I won't. I understand, just know my love for you is undeniable. Please call me if you want." I kissed him on the cheek good-bye before he walked out the door.

I hesitantly closed the door, leaning back with tears flowing from my eyes. Was this it? I couldn't blame him if he wanted to leave me for good. What I did was disrespectful to the fullest and could only blame myself. My strength was slowly leaving my body. There was only one thing I could do. I shook off my weakness and walked over to the sofa and picked up the folder Mark had held in his hand.

As much as I didn't want to believe it, I had to find out. I walked into the bedroom sniffling. I picked up my phone off the floor and started to walk to my office. I scrolled through my contacts searching for our lawyer's number. I opened his contact information and punched in his fax number on my office fax/printer. I placed all the papers in the fax then pressed start. As the fax was connecting, the lawyer's direct line was being dialed.

"Marlon Chapel speaking." His voice was calm.

"Hello, Marlon, how are you? It's Regina Clay."

"Hello, Ms. Clay, what can I do for you? It's been awhile," he greeted me.

"You should be receiving a fax any minute now. Do you have some time to stop by? There's a lot that may happen and I need your expertise."

"Okay, can you hold on a minute?"

I heard him call out to his secretary to retrieve the fax. In a few seconds he returned to the line.

"Ms. Clay, is this what I think it is? Is Mark being—"

"Are the documents real? Is there any way you can find out if the court date is actually a real court hearing?" I bombarded him.

"Tell you what, Ms. Clay, I'll stop over in about an hour or two and then I will be able to answer all your questions."

"Thank you, Marlon, I'll see you then." I hung up the phone praying he would have only one answer: it was all faked. I closed my eyes and silently prayed for just that.

An hour and forty minutes passed as I anxiously waited for the lawyer. I paced back and forth waiting and playing every scenario there would possibly be in my head. Finally, the front desk phone rang. I hurried to pick up. "Hello."

"Hello, Ms. Clay, I have Marlon Chapel here to see you."

"Please send him up right up, thank you." I shuffled quickly to the door and opened it. It felt like eternity, but in a few seconds he arrived walking off the elevator smiling.

"Hello, Ms. Clay, how are you?" He extended his hand.

"Oh, Marlon, I hope I will feel much better after our conversation. Please come in." I returned his smile with a handshake.

"Okay then." He walked in and took a seat at the dining table.

"Can I offer you something to drink?" I took a seat opposite him.

"No, thanks," he said looking around.

A few minutes passed before I realized he was waiting for Mark to enter the room. "Mark is not here so—"

"He's not?" he interrupted.

"Is that a problem?"

He tilted his head a bit and rubbed on his chin as if he was having second thoughts of disclosing whatever information he found out.

"Marlon, there shouldn't be any problem. I'm practically his wife." I hated to remind him.

"You're absolutely right, but I do think he should be here."

"Well, depending on what you tell me I'm sure you will have ample time to go through it all again with him face to face. Shall we get on with it?" I was short with him.

"Of course. The documents are real and the court hearing is on the docket for the scheduled date. Now, I can also tell you the woman making the paternity case is a well-known defense lawyer so this may become very dicey."

"Why, doesn't she get the same treatment as any other paternity case?" I was concerned that Mark would not get a fair trial.

"Yes and no. Because of her ties to the law community this could all be very one-sided or it can be fought word for word by the book. That's why I need to speak to Mark. He has to tell me what happened and if this is at all possible. I'm sure you guys have spoken, but I do need to speak to him. The court date is literally around the corner and I need to prepare my case."

"Is there anything we should do in the meantime?" I asked knowing Mark should be here.

"Well, no contact with the woman and if she does decide on contacting you or Mark please give her my number. Mark and I have to sit down as soon as possible."

"Thank you, Marlon, for taking time out and meeting me. I'm sure Mark will contact you once he returns." I stood up indicating our conversation was over and it was time for him to leave.

"Okay, I guess I'll be on my way, Ms. Clay."

I walked him to the door and thanked him again.

There were a lot of thoughts running through my mind, but I couldn't let it control my actions toward Mark or Amanda. Yes, they did something unforgivable, but the outcome didn't have to suffer. Mark's son shouldn't miss out on his father because his mother didn't make the right decision.

33

Amanda

It felt good to shut Regina's ass up. I was sure she was balling her eyes out right now. Crying over how she could never top me on this; having his kid was the best decision I ever made. There was only one thing left to do: show undeniable proof. His son stayed with my sister in North Carolina at the moment, but he would be here soon enough.

My sister always had my back no matter what; we were blood. There was nothing I wouldn't eventually tell her. I knew I would have to let her in on everything once she arrived, but in the meantime I had to get Tony for what he took part in. Diana shouldn't be hassling me for any more money; she was paid in full first thing this morning. She handed me the flash drive and the hard drive of her personal computer. But I did one better. If she thought I wasn't going to take the hard drive at work she was a step behind me.

Her office computer was replaced before she even sat at her desk this morning.

My private detective got me Tony's full name and address. I didn't know what to expect if he was confronted, but there was no way I was about to let him go that easy. I hopped into a cab reciting his address to the driver. It didn't take long before the cab arrived in front of his building. There wasn't any doorman and the neighborhood was a little sketchy. I handed the driver an extra fifty and told him to hang for fifteen minutes, and if I didn't return it was okay to leave.

I buzzed apartment 3E.

"Who?" a stuffy-nosed voice asked.

"Delivery."

"From who?"

"Is this Tony Lyles?" I asked nervously.

The door buzzed and I entered making sure to slam it behind me then headed to the elevator. *Here we go!* As I entered the elevator I pushed the third-floor button on the panel. There was no turning back now. I got off the elevator and walked down the hall. The door was slightly open. I knocked before I entered.

"You can set it on the table over there. I'll be right there to sign," Tony hollered from the back.

I looked around his apartment littered with empty takeout containers and beer bottles as I walked into the living space. There was a nicely framed picture of a familiar face surrounded by crumpled tissues. *Regina?* This was her Tony! I guessed right when I was at Regina's condo.

"You're not . . . What are you doing here?" He walked out bare-chested and with gym shorts on.

"You know Regina?" I held the picture in my hand.

He was confused. He had no idea I already knew his troubles. I couldn't help but to laugh. I not only fucked her man, I apparently fucked her boyfriend as well. I chuckled to myself. The laugh on Regina just doubled.

"Give me that!" He snatched the frame out my hand. "You don't know her. Listen, I don't know how you got my address, but I'm not on the job anymore. I did you as a favor for a friend."

"You also helped in creating a video to blackmail my ass. Now I need all the footage. So hand it over and I'm out your face."

He walked away and returned with an SD card. "Here, there's nothing else Diana has on you."

"Can I let you in on a little secret?"

"You can leave, that's what you can do," he suggested.

"If you want Regina back maybe you shouldn't give up so quickly. Her man is probably kicking her to the curb right now after finding out that you were fucking her in his bed!"

"How do you know Regina?" he asked anxiously.

"Let's just say I know her better than you think. How I know her doesn't really matter. By the looks of it, you're the only one with a broken heart." I waved my hand around his dirty-ass living room.

"Get out!" he shouted from sheer embarrassment.

"They always say to get over someone the best way is to get under someone else." I winked at him, hoping to comfort his broken heart. This would be just another stab into Regina if I could get Tony again.

"Why are you still talking?"

"Listen, Tony, when we, umm, got together it was under your motives. Now that your motive has been paid in full I would like to offer you another deal under less malicious intentions. You can't deny that it wasn't good."

"I'm listening."

"You being who and what you are, I'm willing to offer you an appropriate fee for your services and an added bonus: access to Regina."

"After what you told me about putting her shit out on blast I would be a fool to believe she'll still have anything to do with you. Stop while you're ahead and leave. I'm not going to make any deal with you even if there was a chance of me getting back Regina. I wasn't born last night!"

I stepped closer to him and gently stroked his bare chest. It would be a shame if I couldn't get him as much as I wanted. "Are you sure? It's not like you're making any money right now."

He pushed my hand off. "Just because I once got paid to fuck you lonely ass bitches for money don't mean I'll be a fish on a hook at any amount."

"Oh, so you have a plan?" I knew he had nothing and only had one skill: fucking.

"What the fuck do you care? Look I've about had it with you. I don't want to force you out physically, but if I have to, trust me, I have no problem in doing it. So, are you leaving on your own or what?" He placed his hands on his hips.

He tried his best to be firm, but when his manhood was standing at full attention it was hard to believe he wanted me to go.

I looked down to his crotch. "I don't think you really want me to leave." Getting what I wanted was never hard. I dropped to my knees and pulled his shorts down. I took him all in. I felt his body relax and his hands moved to the back of my head.

"Yeah, take it all," he moaned.

I slammed my mouth against him causing him to squirm. I sucked harder and jerked my hand faster allowing my spit to drip through my fingers. The wetness formed the perfect glide. He enjoyed every movement my hand made. After his moans became louder I stood up licking my lips.

I wanted what I had that night with him. He knew how I liked it. I smacked him across the face and pushed him to the sofa. His face turned slightly red, but there was a smile brewing.

He pulled my hair hard. "Is this how you want it?" he whispered in my ear.

Instantly my nectar surged. He ripped my blouse open and tugged at my skirt. I had no panties on as usual. When he stuck his hand between my legs my body quivered, wishing he would have his way with me.

"Yes, slap it for me," I groaned.

He tossed me to the other side of the sofa and dove in head first for my flower. He spread me open and nipped at my clitoris. Teasing chills passed through me, feeling the heat from his mouth. His teeth lightly pulling at my clit. It drove me into a fit. I begged and pleaded for him to dig into me, but instead he continued to torment me. I couldn't hold back anymore. I started to squirt all over his face. Tony opened the floodgates ingesting all of my juices and pinching at my nipples.

"Yes, yes. Please, please give it to me."

He teased me for what seemed like hours until he finally climbed on top of me and slammed his ten inches into me. As Tony stroked, his hand around my neck got tighter. The feeling of euphoria came over me and my body shook as I climaxed simultaneously. My body felt light as if I would float away like a helium balloon when my eyes closed.

Suddenly, the door buzzed, jerking me out of my euphoria.

"Who the hell?" Tony cursed. "I swear if you told anybody my address . . ."

The door buzzed again.

"Who?" Tony asked.

"Should hang around for the lady?" the groggy voice came through the intercom.

"Do you have someone waiting on you?" He turned to me and asked removing his finger from the intercom button.

"I can leave if you like. Do you want me to leave?" I spread my legs open.

He pushed the intercom button. "You can go."

I was happy to hear his words. He was willing to play my game for now.

34

Mark

There was so much running through my mind as I slid the keycard into the slot to enter my hotel room. Was I a fool to still love her? Was I so blind? Was Amanda telling me the truth? Did I really have a son? Could I ever forgive the unthinkable? Another man slept with her in my bed, he was in my house. What man in their right mind would forgive her?

I felt exhausted; my body was weak. All the new revelations and the decisions I had to make gave me a horrible headache. It was obvious calling a lawyer would be my next step. Instead, I decided on a hot, steamy shower to calm my mind before calling him.

After my long shower I stepped out of the shower and wrapped one towel around my waist then took the other towel to dry off some more.

I walked to toward the bed to pick up my phone off the nightstand. There were two missed calls, one from Regina and the other from the office. I called the office first.

"Hello, Connie, is there a problem?"

"No, not at all, Mr. Sands, I wanted to check on you. When I called Regina there was no answer." Her kind heart was always uplifting.

"Thanks, Connie, I really appreciate it. I will be out of the office for the rest of the week so please reschedule appointments if necessary."

"Are you not feeling well, Mr. Sands? Would you like me to schedule a doctor's appointment for you?" She was concerned.

"No, not at all. There's some personal matters that need my full attention. Things should settle down by next week." I did my best to sound upbeat and not worry her.

"Okay, Mr. Sands, call me if you need anything."

"I will, Connie, thanks again. Talk to you soon." I pressed End on the phone screen.

As soon as I hung up my phone buzzed. It was Regina.

"Hello," I answered.

"Mark, we need to talk this through and sit with Marlon. He stopped by."

"How did he happen to stop by? Did you call him over?" Not only did she screw people in my bed, but it seemed like she wanted to handle my personal affairs as well.

"I faxed him the documents Amanda left you. I thought you would like to know if they were real moving forward," she stated.

Did she do it for me or was she finding out for her own reasons?

"I found out because we both needed to know if it was true. For you to make sure if this was another trick she had up her sleeve. I needed you to know I was going to be there for you regardless. I'm going to stand by your side. I'm going to help you. We both will be there for your son."

By the sound of her voice she was genuine and compassionate. I didn't want to go through this alone. I loved her, unconditionally, no matter her indiscretions. She was the only one in the world I wanted at my side.

"Mark, where are you?" she asked.

As much as I wanted her next to me, she had to understand her actions almost caused me to walk away. "I still need some time, Regina. I will meet Marlon in the morning and call you after."

"I understand. I'm sorry, Mark. I am, truly. Good-bye," her voice whimpered.

A few tears dropped from my eyes. Her apology was far from winning the trust I once had for her, but it was a start to reviving it. I wiped my eyes and dialed Marlon to set up a very early appointment. When I was done I crawled into bed and slept like a baby.

I woke up, feeling like a better man. I understood my wrongs and had the strength to forgive those for theirs. I left the hotel and hailed a cab to meet Marlon at his office. I replayed in my mind what I was going to say, but it was useless. I knew I made a terrible mistake and it was 100 percent possible Amanda could have mothered my child. As much as I didn't want it to be true, I couldn't fully deny it. I had to face it.

I paid the driver and got out the cab. I entered the building feeling embarrassed by the predicament I was in, but I had to shake that feeling off. I couldn't walk into this feeling like I was in the wrong. She was in the wrong. She kept my son away from me. *I missed some precious moments,* I repeated in my head on the elevator ride up to Marlon's office.

The elevator doors opened and I stepped out onto Marlon's office floor. I walked to the reception area and gave my name.

"Hello, Mr. Sands, Mr. Chapel is expecting you. Please follow me," the young receptionist said.

She led me down a hallway and into a conference room to the left at the end of the hall.

"Can I offer you anything, Mr. Sands? We have fresh coffee, bagels, fruit, and muffins." She gestured to the breakfast feast at the edge of the conference table.

"No, thank you," I offered taking a seat.

"Okay, I'll let Mr. Chapel know you are here."

"Thanks, again." I waited a few minutes anxiously for Marlon to join me. It had been so long since I actually sat down with Marlon I forgot how he looked.

A well-dressed, short, balding, overweight white man walked through the conference doors. "Good morning, Mr. Sands, I only wish it were in better circumstances." He extended his hand.

I gripped his hand still seated. "Thanks for seeing me this early."

"It's only eight in the morning, that's nothing." He took a seat opposite me setting a folder on the table.

"Well, I know you have copies of the document that Amanda Sutton served me yesterday." I looked to his folder.

"Yes, Regina faxed them over to me that very day. I met with her yesterday briefly. Clearly now I can go through the details with you. Can you tell me how these papers were served to you, first?"

"She showed up at my office, but before she entered I stopped her at the door. I did grab her by the arm, not too hard, but thinking back now I probably shouldn't have done it. Anyway once we exited the building she said some harsh words and that moment I thought bringing her to my home was the right thing."

"Why was that, Mark? Were you two lovers for a long time?"

"No, no, no. It was a onetime mistake, that's it. I told Regina the night before that I slept with her a long time ago and Amanda was using her to get closer to me, which Amanda told me herself. I figured we all needed to sit down just to have everything out in the open."

"Were you thinking sitting down with the both of them they were going to become friends again?" His brow rose.

By his expression, that was a stupid move to put them in the same room.

"Forget that question, it doesn't matter. First, we have to address the DNA test. I had my secretary set up the appointment for today. I don't know how your day looks, but I'm sure you will make the adjustment. Now we won't know the results until it's read at the hearing. At that time I can ask for an extension to build a case. Now, I need you to be honest with the some important questions." He rubbed his chin and prepared to write on a legal-sized notepad.

I shook the nervousness off and was ready for all his invading questions. "Yes, I can do that."

"You know Amanda Sutton how exactly?"

"I thought we were friends. We met years ago through some college friends at a party. We kept in contact here and there. After we both were in our careers we continued our friendship with phone calls, e-mails, and occasional dinners. We were friends, so as friends do I confided in her to get a woman's perspective when Regina and I were going through something difficult in our relationship."

"So you've been friends for a long time. Does Regina know her as one of your close friends?"

"No, she didn't. When I made the mistake of sleeping with Amanda I didn't contact her for over a year, maybe even a little more. Then I saw her one night at a client's party. Just by coincidence my client I sold the house to she represented as well. I didn't intend on Regina to find out anything about our previous relationship. When the client brought us together I pretended not to know her. Amanda followed my lead and did the same. Then a week later Regina was meeting her for lunch."

"I see, and Regina never mentioned Amanda saying anything about knowing you?"

"No. If she was ever at the house, I left to do something or locked myself away in my home office. I didn't do dinners with her unless Regina insisted, which she did at times." I felt like shit reliving this.

"And she never mentioned a baby to Regina or you?"

"No."

He wrote on the notepad for quite a few minutes before looking up to me again. "Okay, do you intend to be in his child's life if you're the father?"

"Yes, I wouldn't want it any other way."

"If you're not are you prepared to press charges and file a restraining order against her?"

"Yes."

"Okay, I think I have some work to do and you my friend have an appointment. The young lady at the front desk will give all the information to you." He pushed back on his chair and stood up extending his hand to me.

"That's it, nothing else?" I shook his hand and rose out the seat.

"For now. The main thing is the test, after we can build a stronger case."

"You know she's a lawyer, right?" He didn't mention anything and honestly I was uncertain of his skill.

"Of course I do. Mark, don't worry about this. It will work out." He stated with a smile.

His words didn't make me confident, but he was head of his firm and I was sure he didn't want his reputation to be tarnished in any way. I walked to the reception area and the receptionist handed me a manila folder with all the information in it. I thanked her and headed to the elevator to exit the building. I hailed a cab once I was out and headed to the appointment.

After waiting almost two hours to have my cheek swabbed and blood taken I was finally sitting in a cab on my way back to the hotel. Once I got into my room I ordered some much-needed lunch. As I waited for my lunch, I picked up my phone and dialed Regina.

"Hello," she answered.

"I saw Marlon this morning and went to get the DNA test today."

"It had to be done. Did he mention what was to be done at this hearing coming up?" She had every right to be concerned.

"He said we wouldn't get the DNA results until the hearing then he would ask for some more time to build a case."

"That's it?" she asked sounding disappointed.

"The court date is a day from tomorrow. I would like you to be there with me."

"Of course, Mark. Can—"

There was a strong knock on the door. "Regina, I'll see you at the hearing. We'll talk then, I promise." I pressed End on the screen while opening the door.

"Room service, sir," a bellhop announced handing me the bill to sign off.

"Thank you," I said penning in his tip and my signature on bill.

I sat there and ate with my thoughts of the future filling my head.

35

Amanda

I was familiar with the court building when I entered and already knew where to go. I pushed the stroller carrying little Mark as my sister followed. When I pushed through the door labeled ROOM 1602, I saw Mark seated with his lawyer and Regina sitting behind him. He stared at us, probably hoping to sneak a peek at his son, I thought, striding to my seat.

"Don't remove the blanket, and make sure he stays quiet," I whispered into my sister's ear.

"All rise for the Honorable Judge Janet Thomas," the bailiff announced.

The judge took her seat and greeted us. "Good morning, my good folks. Let's see what we have here." She looked over some papers in front of her.

Both lawyers stood up to address the judge. "Good morning, Your Honor," they said in unison.

"Okay, I see we have an order of paternity." She continued to look through the papers before her.

"Yes, Mr. Sands has executed the request. The results were sent directly to you, Your Honor," Mark's lawyer informed the judge.

"Yes, yes, I see that. I do have the results. Mr. Mark Sands." She looked to him as he stood up.

"You are the father by 99.9 percent certainty. Now, are you seeking joint custody at this time?"

Mark looked to his lawyer then back at the judge. "Yes, at this moment."

"Does that mean you will be filing for full custody in the future?"

"Yes, Your Honor," Mark answered.

"We would like to request of the court a temporary joint custody with an immediate unsupervised visit starting today. My client has yet to meet his son, Your Honor," Mark's lawyer interjected.

The judge grabbed a pen and wrote something down on the paper in front of her before looking up to address us. "Okay, I grant the visitation immediately after this hearing in the family room down the hall for two hours."

I finally stood up and whispered into my lawyer's ear, "Object to the visit. I don't want his visitation unsupervised."

My lawyer did as he was told and objected to the visitation.

"Ms. Sutton, is there a reason you would not like an unsupervised visit? There's no abuse charges in this case."

"I think by me being there it would be a better transition. As his mother, I just want the best for my son," I answered.

"From all the statements before me, I don't think it matters if you are there or not. From the looks of it here your sister has been the only mother he's known since you gave birth to him. What's best for your son, you clearly proved that you aren't by my standard, which is also the court's. Your sister along with both opposing lawyers will supervise the visit today. Moving forward, all visitation will not require your presence."

"But—"

The judge banged her gavel to silence me.

"Mr. Sands, I grant you three weekly unsupervised visits for five hours each until your next hearing. Mr. Chapel, you and your client will produce a schedule for the next month after the visitation today. Ms. Sutton, you are not to contact Mr. Sands for any reason. If you need to address any issues, please address his lawyer and vice versa. If either of you chose not to abide by these restrictions, you both will be back in my courtroom facing my wrath. Do all sides understand?"

"Yes, Your Honor," I spoke through clenched teeth.

"Great, see you in a month." The judge slammed her gavel down and turned to the bailiff to discuss the next court date.

I was infuriated. I was sure the judge was going to allow me to be there. I provided all the affidavits to show the judge I was setting up a home for little Mark. I gave documents of the new house I bought out in New Jersey. The private nurse and nanny I hired to be around while little Mark was in my care. I didn't get it. It sure as hell wasn't supposed to go down this way.

"Ms. Sutton, please follow me." The bailiff escorted me to a secluded room where I sat for two hours while my sister introduced my son to his father. It all backfired on me and now this verdict from the judge cut into me a little deeper.

I paced the floor, played games on my phone, spoke to several clients to pass the time. Finally the same bailiff walked in with my lawyer and Mark's lawyer. Where was little Mark? I looked and saw little Mark on Regina's lap with Mark smiling beside her outside in the hallway as the doors closed behind the lawyers. They looked happy. All of them.

"Ms. Sutton, please have a seat."

I preferred not to. My skin was on fire with anger. "No, thank you."

"We have scheduled visits for the next month. We just need your signature on the dotted line," Mark's lawyer stated pushing in front of me.

"No, fucking way! I see you forgot to mention to the judge how unfit his girlfriend was! I do not want her near or caring for my son. She has an addiction sleeping with random men and bringing them into their home."

My lawyer tried to calm me down; then the bailiff walked in. "Is there a problem in here?"

"Yes, can we see the judge in chambers please?"

The bailiff picked up the phone in the room and spoke into the receiver covering his mouth. After a few minutes, we were all led into the judge's chambers.

"This can't be good." The judge put her robe on and sat at the desk. We all took a seat in front of her.

"I don't want his girlfriend around my son," I blurted out.

The judge stared at me. "Calm down, Ms. . . ."

"Sutton." I rolled my eyes.

"Ms. Sutton, what is your reasoning?"

"She's a sex addict and allows prostitutes in the same home as Mark." I exposed Regina's dirty secret.

"How might you know that?"

"Because, she's told me."

"Was this after or before you told her you had a son by Mr. Sands?"

I had to lay it on thick. I swore to fire my lawyer as soon as we left the judge because it was obvious I was fighting with no help. "I didn't want my son to be in those circumstances. Mark works all the time and I knew she would be the one looking after him. How do I know she wouldn't bring some stranger into her house when my son is there? I was scared, wouldn't you be?"

Just then Mark and Regina walked into the room.

"Your Honor, can we say a few words, please?"

I didn't know what to say or do. I was uncomfortable.

"Mr. Sands, and who might this be?"

"This is my future wife, Regina Clay. We will be married soon."

"Nice to meet you, Ms. Clay. I've been told you have an addiction? Is this true?"

Regina's eyes widened and her face turned red. "No addiction, just decisions I choose not to make anymore. Without going into detail I was unfaithful to Mark and have since changed my ways. When I first learned about this I was mad and resented Amanda. Now, I can't even think about that resentment because she has given us, Mark, something I will never be able to provide him."

"You can't have kids?" the judge asked.

"Correct. I would have to have a surrogate carry our child."

"Your Honor, may I speak?" Mark grabbed Regina's hand then continued, "We have been through a lot lately and with all of this out in the open, it's put everything in perspective for us."

I stifled myself with curses in my mind. *Don't tell me she's falling for this bullshit!*

"What's that, Mr. Sands?"

"After meeting with my son, it was unbelievable that I missed out on his first months of his life. I don't want to miss anything else. Regina and I have agreed to counseling on a weekly basis to ensure our impending marriage will be honest and a great home for little Mark to be a part of."

He turned my stomach while I listened to his pathetic plea in front of the judge.

"Your Honor, I can't be certain she will stick to not being a whore!"

"Ms. Sutton, please refrain from using that sort of language. You're a lawyer, please respect my chambers."

"Your Honor, I can undoubtly tell you I trust Regina and that's more than I can say about Amanda, honestly."

Regina squeezed Mark's hand as if to tell him to ease up.

"Everyone out of my chambers except for the lawyers," she said.

I stormed out the judge's chambers with every intention of grabbing little Mark and heading straight out the building. But when I looked back the bailiff was standing outside the judge's chambers. *Fuck!* I cursed silently. *This was supposed to be easy!* I kept thinking. Regina and Mark stood close to the bailiff opposite where little Mark was. My sister sat on the bench with me and had little Mark on her lap. He was squirming around stretching his hands out, then went into a sure fit kicking and crying.

Mark looked to the bailiff as if asking if he could take the child to help soothe him. The bailiff gestured to go ahead.

I wanted to jump up and snatch little Mark right out his hand, but as soon as his son into his arms he stopped. He calmed immediately. At that exact moment my anger and frustration dissipated. I saw the bond already formed in such a short time between the two of them. There was love, genuine love. The love I'd been searching for. I realized I would never have that kind of love if I continued with my games. Looking at Regina playing and making little Mark laugh I knew what I was doing wasn't going to help the situation for him. For the first time in my life choosing to do the right thing without any malice behind it was easier to swallow. I stood up and walked over to the bailiff. "Tell my lawyer to give him whatever he wants." I turned around and walked toward the staircase to exit the building.

There were no tears, no remorse of what I'd done to Mark and Regina. I felt walking out would tell them I was done with the games. I had to do right by my son even if it meant giving him up to Mark and Regina. He deserved to be loved, genuinely.

36

Regina

The day was finally here. Our wedding day. After all the drama with Amanda we needed this more than ever. We had made a united front ensuring Amanda's half-truths and chaos couldn't affect our relationship again. When I took a stand that night by forcing her out of our home it all became clear. If Mark and I allowed her to take control she would forever play her games with our lives more than she already was.

I had to come to terms and respected that Mark had a child with this woman, but I sure as hell wasn't going to allow her to dictate our future moving forward. Yes, she had to be in our lives, but we weren't going to be a part of her schemes. When Mark received joint custody it was made clear there would be no contact with us by her; everything had to go through our lawyers. When she left the courthouse and allowed us to take little Mark, she did the right thing. The judge wasn't shocked and granted him immediate custody until Mark and I were legally married and told me to file for adoption. I didn't want Amanda to be pulled away from little Mark, but maybe it was the best thing to do.

"Regina, it's time." Mema entered my suite with the happiest smile on her face.

I wore an off-white, simple off-the-shoulder full-length dress with a small train. My hair was pinned up with a fresh floral headpiece created from the garden. My face was covered slightly with netting.

Mark spared no expense on making sure this day was perfect for me. He rented out an entire house overlooking the beach at one of the ritziest resorts in Cabo San Lucas, Mexico. There was a butler on call at all times, a chef to prepare anything we wanted to eat; we didn't have to alter anything. They made sure everything was perfect from sunrise to sundown.

"Are you ready?" Mema asked again.

I checked my hair, makeup, and gown in the full-length mirror in front of me.

"You look absolutely gorgeous!" Mema complimented me.

I blushed. "Thanks, Mema. Where's little Mark?"

"Mark wanted his son at his side at the altar. I hope you don't mind."

"Not at all. I'm committing myself to the both of them today and wouldn't have it any other way." A joyful tear dropped from my eye.

"Don't cry, it's everything you wanted, everything you deserve. Come on, what are you waiting for? Let's go get you married!"

She was so happy and I was just happy she was by my side. "I love you, Mema, I do." I hugged her so tight.

"I love you too, Regina, unconditionally." She unwrapped her arms and pointed to the open French doors. There was a white tent preventing Mark from seeing me when I walked over the threshold. I took my spot and waited.

I snuck a little peek when Mema walked through the tent onto the beach. The beach was set up beautifully. Colored flowers littered each side of the aisle I was to walk down. There were no chairs set up for guests because there were none. I decided the only people who should be there would be our family: Mema, little Mark, and us. There was even a stage set up with a live band. I figured it was for my grand entrance.

As I stood there waiting there were no nerves plaguing me, no worries that Amanda would somehow ruin everything, there was just peace and pure happiness. I was about to marry the man of my dreams. Suddenly, I heard the music. The tent was opened and I made my descent to the beach as the band played the traditional bridal song. When I stepped onto the beach the music changed. I was brought to tears when I heard John Legend singing "All of Me" as I walked down the aisle to both Marks. *Damn, my makeup is going to look like a mess!*

For some reason I didn't care as long as they were in my life forever.

Epilogue

After Mark and Regina made their everlasting commitment to each other on a secluded beach in Mexico, Regina officially adopted little Mark. It was everything she wanted, from her wedding to the unconditional love Mark proclaimed.

It didn't take long for Regina to fall into motherhood; somehow it came to her with Mema there to help. Regina never wanted to deny Mark the one thing in life he most desired. She didn't have to fight within herself to stay true to Mark or her promise before God. Regina didn't want anything or anyone to come between Mark and her again. It was her mission to be the best mother for little Mark and the best wife to Mark.

Amanda made no effort to see or ask about little Mark, which made her intentions clear. A few days after the first hearing her lawyer contacted them about her future role in her son's life: she wanted nothing to do with him. It was sad that she thought using her son to force a man permanently into her life would somehow work.

Diana received her extorted money from Amanda and left the job and city she loved hoping for a new start. She realized her past mistakes and thought she'd better start making amends before karma showed its ugly head without sympathy. She moved halfway across the world to put the much-needed distance from her past and unwanted acquaintances.

Tony realized his worth to Amanda and Regina: simply nothing, but satisfaction in the bedroom. After his second run-in with Amanda, he didn't want anything to do with her. She tried her very best to offer him tons of money for his affection, but he wouldn't have it. He understood with a woman like that there was no room for others whether they paid him or not. She had no self-worth if every time they met his hands had to leave her bruised. He wanted nothing to do with that and didn't want her capable of pinning any false accusations on him. Tony eventually went back to his career and the only skill he had to make money. The lonely housewives and unwanted uglies of the city kept him busy.

In the end Regina got what she wanted: a marriage with unconditional love and adornment without expectations. Now all she had to do was uphold her newfound devotion to her husband and her son.

Coming soon

Girls From da Hood 11

a novella by

Natalie Weber

Prologue

I need it. I want it. Why shouldn't I have it? I shouldn't be here. I just want a little. Who will it hurt? My mind and body floated away. There was nothing I could do to save myself from myself. I grabbed the lightly tinted small blue bag out of his hand and rushed into the house they happily provided for me to shelter my behavior away from spying eyes. But I knew better. I felt the eyes of many burning through the back of my head. I wasn't deterred from doing me.

I entered the house rushing toward one of the back rooms. My arms, legs, neck began to itch as it normally would when I needed to get back on track without getting sick. There were no doors on any of the rooms in the house. The stench alone would run any normal person in the opposite direction. I was far from normal— now. I hunkered down in the far corner from the entrance of the room. There wasn't much light.

Quickly I pulled out my works and started to assemble my fix.

Once my needle was filled with the toxic fluid I stabbed my vein willingly. Happy to feel the pain and euphoria at the same time. My eyes closed slowly allowing the powerful drug to take a hold of my body. I felt nothing but peace, happiness, love and most of all—if not the best part—there was no noise. No one screaming at me to stop. No one banging on the door to gain entry to stop me. It was just me. It was all me.

I must have dozed off because a strong kick to the face shook me out of my nod. There was nothing I could do. I covered my bleeding face and braced myself for another blow.

"Yo, what the fuck you doin'? Leave that junky-bitch alone. Let's get this money and bounce. Let's go!" a familiar voice said.

I didn't dare to look or even remove my hands from my face. I played my role to stay alive. It was obvious now that these fools were robbing the joint. I wanted to open my eyes to see where my works went immediately after the 'kick a bitch in the head' moment.

I only heard an eerie laughter, almost as if he enjoyed it. I didn't move, not even a grimace spilled from my mouth.

In the next moment I heard feet shuffling out of the room. Slowly I opened my eyes, still using my hands as a barrier just in case the joke was on me again. My eyes darted around the floor in front of me and thank goodness I spotted my works. I listened carefully before making my move.

I still heard voices so I figured they were just in the adjacent hallway. Suddenly the voices got louder. Instinctively my body tucked into a fetal position against the wall.

"You bitch-ass! You tryin'a to hold out? You must be gettin' paid a whole lot of fuckin' money to risk yo' life. I'm just gonna ask one more time. Where the fuck is the safe?"

"That's all . . . you got everything. We was s'pose to get restocked today. The money was picked up this mor'in' . . ."

I heard a big thump hit the floor. It made me jump.

Damn, niggas sing like birds when they life on the line. No loyalty to no one only themselves. My thoughts were just that—thoughts. I knew if I was in the same position my ass would be singing like a humming bird. I wanted to get the fuck up out of there, though. They sure as hell sobered my ass up quickly. *Fuck! Fuck! Fuck!* I cursed in my head.

"A'ight, when they comin'?"

There was silence for a brief moment.

"It's four now . . . they s'pose to be here now."

Suddenly there was a loud bang. It sounded like a shot gun—the kind that leaves a soccer ball-sized hole in your chest.

Automatically I shot up and grabbed my works off the floor and hurried to an open closet. Of course there was no door on it, but it was better than being an open target. At least I was somewhat hidden if anyone looked into the room.

Within seconds there was a flurry of gun shots that rang out. I almost soiled my pants because of fear. *I can't die like this. Anything but this . . . God, please . . .* Praying, pleading, begging to be rescued from this nightmare was all I could do. I closed my eyes and prayed it would be over quickly.

The Beginning

"Thank you for flying with JetSuite, it's been a pleasure."

I was a bit groggy from whatever Sterling gave me to calm my nerves to put me out for most of the flight. I've never been on a plane before so I was a little more than nervous. I looked out the window and saw that we already landed. *Thank God!* Thank goodness I wasn't up for the landing, I almost crapped my pants when we took off.

"Hey you, it's time to go. We're here."

I was so happy he chose me. Sterling had his choice of anyone including his girl of two years. They was wrong when everyone said being a side chick had no benefits. I tried to stand up but felt dizzy and plopped back down in the seat.

"You a'ight?" He sounded concerned. "Hold on, we'll wait," he said reaching into the overhead compartment.

I sure as hell didn't want him to think I wasn't down. I forced myself to my feet and strongly held on to the back of the chair in front of me.

He pulled out our matching Rawlings duffle bags and placed them in the seat. We entered the aisle behind the crowd exiting.

"Thank you, for flying JetSuite," the stewardess said as we exited the plane.

"Thank you, the flight was great," I said knowing I was asleep the entire flight. The stewardess gave me a fake smile and happy nod.

Now why in the world would I say that? I looked to Sterling and by his expression on his face I knew I should've kept my mouth shut. We walked off the plane down a long narrow lighted hallway to a line flashing a green light.

"Is this Puerto Rico?" I asked quietly.

"Nah, we in D.R. It's the hottest place to be. Wait 'til you see where we stayin'!" His words made me excited.

"How are we gettin' there?" I asked feeling stupid once the question left my mouth.

He looked around. "Give me a kiss."

I did.

"I can't believe how lucky I am. This gonna be somethin' you'll never forget, trust me."

I smiled and hugged on Sterling's arm. I noticed two dogs at the front of the line. It didn't dawn on me that it was drug dogs until I saw Sterling's face. I hugged him tight and whispered in his ear, "We good?"

We walked slowly to the counter. Sterling handed over our passports with a smile, just then the dogs were called to another counter. The relief on Sterling's face worried me.

"Enjoy your stay," the man said stamping our passports.

We exited the airport bombarded with people selling jewelry, food, drinks out of their make-shift cubicles. They all spoke Spanish so I didn't understand a word.

There was a driver waiting for us with Sterling's name on a sign. He was standing in front of something like a mini party bus. I was more than impressed.

"Mr. Sterling, welcome! Can I get your bags?" A tall, pale looking man greeted us.

"I got this," Sterling clenched the straps of the bag.

"No problem, there's champagne chilling in the car," the driver tipped his chauffeur hat and opened the door.

"Damn, you went all out for our weekend, huh?"

"Hell yeah," he stepped onto the party bus doing his cute little happy dance like he always did when he was feeling himself.

I followed behind him stifling my excitement. I saw the floor and interior was lit up with neon lights, it even had a bar and two huge flat screen TVs, and the windows reflected no light from the outside. Once inside the smell of luxury opened my eyes wide, it was scented with the smell of money. The plush butter-soft white leather seats seduced my body into complete relaxation when I took a seat.

"Okay, Mr. Sterling, have fun we will arrive at the resort in two hours."

"Thanks," Sterling said tossing his bag onto one of the seats.

"Pop that champagne, baby, let's get it!" I stood up and did my twerk dance, bouncing my round plump ass just how he liked it.

"Girl, you better stop that . . ." he rubbed his crotch.

All the windows were tinted on the bus so it was easy to peer out without worrying about anyone seeing me. I lifted my leg to one of the seats and poked my ass out taunting him.

"Girl, you better get over here and give me some of that," he said smacking me on my ass.

I giggled as he grabbed me and held me close. He kissed on my lips and my neck, I felt him rising beneath me. I started to grind on him slowly. I had to make him want me around and this trip proved it. This was the first time he'd ever included me in this part of his life; he trusted me.

"You want it, baby?" I whispered although, I knew the answer.

"You gonna give it to me right here? Right now?" he was surprised

"Why not? We are on vacation ain't we?" I reached for his belt buckle to release his nine inches. I got up soon after and pulled my underwear down quickly; the reason I wore the skirt, easy access. I climbed over him and eased my way down feeling his stiffness fully.

"Damn . . . you feel so good," he moaned.

I started to rotate my hips speeding up my movement as his moans got louder. He managed to pull my tank top up to suck and twist on my nipples; my most loved style of foreplay.

"Yes baby . . . suck on them . . ."

Feeling his tongue circling my hard nipple made my clit throb. I loved feeling the hot air from his mouth on my skin. He pumped into me harder with each stroke. I loved feeling him inside me. He did me like no other man had. With each stroke he knew where to hit to make me moan louder and louder. Suddenly, he stopped.

"Hey, not fair," I whined.

"Be quiet," he said through clenched teeth.

There was something wrong. The party bus was no longer moving. I looked out the window and we were pulled over to the side of the dirt road. I fixed myself quickly and looked over to Sterling. He pointed to the bag. I got down low and crawled to where the bag was. It must have fell while we were getting it on. I waited for him to make a move.

There was a light knock at the door. "Mr. Sterling?"

Sterling reached for the bag and opened it. He pulled out two plastic 9 mm guns.

"What the fuck is going on?" I questioned in a low voice.

"I don't know, but we about to find out." He tossed one of the guns to me.

I gave him the crazy look. "How we gonna kill anybody with these?"

"Let's find out." He cocked the gun ready for anything.

I trusted him, but I still feared the worst.